"Walt Williams is back in the 6th installment of the Lady Justice series.

This time, Walt and his partner, Ox, are looking into the case of assisted suicide.

When an ALS patient dies, his daughter is not sure if it's of natural causes. Soon, they find out that someone had assisted in his death. They are on the trail of a man who they are calling 'Dr. Death'.

This is a controversial subject and the book brings out both sides of the issue. Some feel Dr. Death is a hero, putting terminal patients out of their misery and allowing them to die with dignity. Others feel he is a cold-blooded murderer.

Walt is faced with these moral issues in one of his toughest cases yet.

All of the lovable characters are back and they are faced with their own mortality.

Filled with laugh-out-loud comedy, danger and suspense, Mr. Thornhill brings up a sensitive subject in a unique and satisfying way.

A thought provoking and satisfying read with a perfect ending.

If I could only read one book this year, this would be my choice!"

Sheri Wilkinson (Goodreads)

1

"I love it when authors use the genre of fiction to raise awareness of issues the general public should be more aware of.

I've long known that we have corruption and collusion in our government, and it's nice to see it be more exposed in an accessible manner.

Euthanasia, which is the main focus of this novel, is a touchy subject to deal with. However, the author, Robert Thornhill, does it in a way that presents all sides fairly and evenly.

I don't want to spoil the ending by telling you how it ended. I think that your personal views notwithstanding, you'll appreciate the ending.

Nothing about this short novel bored me. Thornhill moved through the plot efficiently without wasting the reader's time.

Overall, this was a thoughtful novel with plenty of character and intrigue to keep the reader engaged."

April Rabian (Goodreads)

LADY JUSTICE

AND

DR. DEATH

**A WALT WILLIAMS
MYSTERY/COMEDY NOVEL**

ROBERT THORNHILL

Lady Justice and Dr. Death
Copyright September, 2011 by Robert Thornhill.
All rights reserved.

Published in the United States of America

Cover design by Peg Thornhill

1. Fiction, Humorous
2. Fiction, Mystery & Detective, General

FORWARD

While this novel is a work of fiction, many elements of the story are based in fact.

Walt's skirmishes with the Food and Drug Administration in *Lady Justice and Dr. Death* are based on actual accounts of raids by the FDA on both a bread manufacturer and the producer of bottled elderberry juice.

You may read more about these incidents at:
http://healthfreedoms.org/2011/06/10/elderberry-juice-drug-raid/ and
http://www.hcgweightloss.com/chapter-4-who-are-they/

Robert and Kay Gordon are the owners of Gordon's Orchard in Osceola, Mo. and the 'Bob Gordon Elderberry' does exist.

For the full story, go to:
http://www.elderberryalliance.org/documents/ByersPatrick.pdf

That such conspiracies exist in real life is something that most of us would choose not to believe, but sometimes, the truth is stranger and even more unbelievable than fiction.

LADY JUSTICE AND DOCTOR DEATH

PROLOGUE

The life of eighty-six year old Roger Beckham had been as full as any man could have hoped for.

His parents were warm and supportive and he had many fond childhood memories.

He was the first in his family to graduate from college and he was fortunate to have gotten into the ground floor of the growing dot com industry.

His wife of forty years had given him two lovely daughters and they, in turn, had given him three doting grandchildren.

Of course there were adjustments after his wife passed away ten years ago, but for a man of means, life was still good.

He loved to travel, enjoy good food, vintage wine, an occasional fine cigar and now and then, the company of a lovely young lady.

All that changed six months ago.

He had begun to feel tired and out-of-sorts, not his usual self, so he scheduled a checkup.

After a round of tests, Dr. Billings gave him the news that brought his world crashing down around him.

He had cancer.

Not just any cancer, but the aggressive kind that had rapidly metastasized and spread throughout his internal organs.

Encouraged by his family to fight the deadly disease, he began a rigorous round of radioactive treatments and chemotherapy.

The treatment had taken its toll.

His hair was gone, he had lost thirty pounds and, worst of all, he had lost his will to live.

He could no longer travel, his food, no matter how tasty, would come back up and even the thought of female companionship had lost its allure.

His doctor had assured him that the treatments could prolong his life for another six months, maybe even a year if he was lucky.

Lucky!

He had perused the Internet and read the

pamphlets, so he knew what was coming.

Soon he would be confined to his bed; then would come the catheter and intravenous feeding and finally the morphine drip that would ease the pain through the final weeks.

Not only had he lost his health, but he would lose his dignity as well.

But he discovered that even a dying man has options if he is well connected.

He made some discreet inquiries and was directed to a man that he came to know only as 'Thanatos'.

The initial contacts with the man were much like the first meeting between a 'john' and a high-priced hooker.

Each knows what the other wants, but neither wants to come right out and say it just in case one of them is a cop.

Finally, after a very painful night, Beckham called Thanotos.

"I want to die! Can you help me?"

"I can, but you have to do exactly as I say."

The first thing that Thanatos had done was to get Beckham to change physicians.

He switched to Dr. Graves under the premise that the new doctor had some different treatment options.

Then he presented Beckham with a written questionnaire requiring specific answers as to why he wanted to die, and finally, he signed a declaration asking for euthanasia and absolving Thanatos and all parties connected with the act, of any coercion or wrongdoing.

That was a month ago and at last the time had arrived.

Beckham lived alone and he had chosen a night when he knew that his family would be occupied, so that there would be no interruptions.

Thanatos had encouraged Beckham to create a computer disk of things and places that had been important to him in his life and to select his favorite music.

When he arrived, Thanatos directed Beckham to relax in his recliner, with his computer close at hand.

He sat a small folding table beside the recliner on which he placed a machine with three vials connected to an IV tube.

Another line running from the machine was connected to a toggle switch.

"This is how it will work," Thanatos said. "I will connect this IV tube to a syringe that I will insert into your vein.

"When you are ready, simply press the toggle

switch to activate the machine.

"The first chemical to enter your system will put you to sleep; the second will relax your muscles and the third will deliver the relief you have been seeking.

"This is your time, so take as much time as you need. Enjoy your video and your music.

"I will leave you to be alone with your thoughts."

"What about my family?" Beckham asked.

"When you have finished, I will remove everything connected to your final act. Your family will simply believe that you passed away during the night."

Beckham looked deep into Thanatos' eyes. "Thank you for this; for letting me die with dignity."

Thanatos smiled with genuine compassion. "That's what we do."

Thanatos left the room and Beckham turned on the computer.

Images of his childhood, his early years, his wife and his children passed before his eyes while the notes of Elvis' haunting *Memories* filled the room.

The only thing that could have been more perfect was if his daughters and grandchildren could have been with him in his last moments, but with the laws as they were, he knew that it could never be.

He quietly sang along:

"Quiet thoughts come floating down and settle softly to the ground, like golden autumn leaves around my feet.

"I touch them and they burst apart with sweet memories. Sweet memories."

A photo of him and his wife on their wedding day filled the screen and he pressed the toggle switch.

His last words were, "I'm coming, dear. I'm coming."

Thanatos returned and seeing Beckham slumped in the recliner, felt for a pulse.

There was none.

Quietly, he removed the IV from Beckham's arm, packed his machine and put the computer away.

He looked around the room.

When Beckham's family found him, they would believe that he had passed peacefully in his sleep.

He slipped out the door and disappeared into the night.

CHAPTER 1

The life of a cop is mostly the same boring, routine stuff day after day, punctuated by interludes of adrenaline-pumping excitement and, sometimes, near death experiences.

The 'near-death' thing was fresh in my mind having just survived an assassination attempt by a hired killer.

We had just wrapped up a 'sting' operation involving a large pharmaceutical company and corrupt politicians, so I was more than ready for a few days of the 'boring' stuff.

My partner, Ox, and I were on routine patrol in our old black and white Crown Vic.

Ox and I had been together almost three years and riding with him was as comfortable as wearing an old shoe.

Not many cops with Ox's twenty-plus years on the force would have wanted to be paired with a sixty-five year old rookie, but he had taken it in stride and somehow, it had worked.

The unlikely combination of Ox's two hundred and twenty pounds and twenty years on the streets and my hundred and forty-five pound body, with gray hair and seemingly incredible good luck, had compiled quite an arrest record.

We were cruising just south of the Country Club Plaza when the radio came to life.

"Car 54. What's your twenty?"

Ox keyed the mike. "Car 54. We're at Fifty-fifth and Wornall."

"Proceed to the eighty-four hundred block of Holmes Avenue. The family called in a death."

"Understood. We're on the way."

Most people don't realize that every death that occurs outside a medically supervised facility requires a police investigation, and there are a lot of them.

Now that I have reached the ripe old age of sixty-eight, I find myself paying more attention to the obituaries in the *Kansas City Star*.

Every day there are thirty to sixty new listings.

Once in a while, I will see an old classmate or

13

a client to whom I sold a house during my thirty-year real estate career.

It always brings back memories and I always feel sad.

I don't know why I do it.

On an average, Ox and I respond to two to four calls a week involving a dead body.

Thankfully, none, so far, have been people I know.

Most are simply the result of a natural death caused by illness or trauma. Some are suicides and, of course, the occasional murder.

Our job is to try to determine which of those occurred and respond accordingly.

This is the part of the job that I dislike the most.

Death is never a pleasant time under any circumstances.

Even when it is the result of natural causes, the family is wracked with grief.

In suicide and murder, disbelief and anger are thrown in with the grief.

I have always had great respect for those whose professions require them to deal with death on a continual basis, the doctors and nurses and staff in nursing homes, to name just a few.

We pulled up in front of the Holmes Avenue

address.

Two cars and an ambulance were already there.

An EMT met us at the door.

"What have we got?" Ox asked.

"An old guy, in his eighties. One daughter found him this morning. She called her sister and then us. They're with him now.

"His name is Roger Beckham. He was in the last stages of cancer. Looks like he died around midnight."

The two sisters were consoling one another when we entered the room.

"I'm Officer Williams and this is Officer Wilson. We're sorry for your loss."

"Thank you. I'm Willa Parker and this is my sister Mary Payne. We knew it was coming, but I guess you're never ready."

"I understand," I said. "Who is Mr. Beckham's doctor?"

"Uhhh --- Dr. Graves. I have his number here."

"My partner has a few more questions for you while I call Dr. Graves."

I dialed the number and was transferred.

"Dr. Graves. This is Officer Williams with the Kansas City Police Department. We're at the home of

Roger Beckham. He passed away during the night. I understand that he was one of your patients."

"Indeed he was. He fought a valiant fight --- cancer, you know."

"Yes, that's what we were told. So you'll sign the death certificate?"

"Of course."

"Thanks for your time."

I returned to Ox and the sisters.

"Dr. Graves is on board with the death certificate, so we can release the body. Where would you like him taken?"

"After he was diagnosed, he made all the arrangements himself so that we wouldn't have to," Willa said. "He has arranged for cremation at Newcomers, so I guess he can be taken there.

"Can we take a moment to say 'good bye'?"

"Of course."

The EMT was waiting outside.

"Funeral home or morgue?" he asked.

"Funeral home. Newcomers. The doctor signed off."

In my early days on the force, I had been surprised to learn that any death that was not signed off by a doctor, required that the body be transported to the morgue where the coroner would establish cause of death.

Most of the examinations were cursory, but occasionally, when the circumstances surrounding the death were in question, there would be a complete autopsy.

We wrapped things up at the Beckham home and resumed our regular patrol.

Neither of us spoke. We were each immersed in our own thoughts.

Death will do that.

I was mostly past my 'death funk' by the time I got home that evening.

I try my best to not bring my work home to my sweet wife, Maggie, but so far, that hadn't been working out too well.

We've been a couple for many years, but living together as husband and wife, less than a year.

We had worked together at City Wide Realty until I retired and got the bright idea to become a cop.

Maggie has supported me all the way.

I'm guessing that she didn't realize, when she said, "I do, for better or for worse," that the 'for worse' part would include being abducted, kidnapped and nearly shot.

I suppose any relationship is filled with surprises, but most don't include murder and mayhem.

In our most recent narrow escape, a hired assassin was holding Maggie and me at gunpoint and was about to pull the trigger.

The day had been saved by our old friend, Mary Murphy, who took out the bad guy with one swing of her thirty-six inch, white ash baseball bat.

The Bible has its story of a giant being taken out by a shepherd boy with a slingshot.

We've got Mary Murphy and her bat.

Mary manages my Three Trails Hotel.

I own it, but I'm not proud of it.

There are twenty sleeping rooms sharing four hall baths, plus Mary's small apartment.

Its occupants are mostly old retired guys on Social Security or men with questionable job skills that work out of the labor pool.

Let's face it; it's all they can afford.

An old friend of mine is fond of saying, "Well, everybody's got to be somewhere." These guys might as well be there.

Even at the age of seventy-three, Mary is an imposing figure.

She has the demeanor of a pit bull. That,

along with her two hundred pounds and her bat, makes her the perfect housemother to my twenty misfits.

Maggie and I had been worried about Mary.

After dropping the assassin with one fell swoop, Mary had collapsed into my arms and wept.

I'm still not sure if the tears were tears of relief that we were safe or tears of regret that she had taken a life.

Even professionals, with years of experience in law enforcement, have difficulty coming to grips with the realization they had taken a life.

Officers are encouraged to seek counseling from the department's psychologist and that service was offered to Mary, but she politely refused.

We decided to drop by and see if Mary was doing all right.

When we pulled up in front of the hotel, Lawrence Wingate was just leaving.

Lawrence is the one exception to the motley crew that inhabits the hotel.

He is actually a well-educated computer technician who got cleaned out by a bitchy wife and had to start life from scratch.

"Walt. Maggie. How's it going?" he asked.

"Great, Lawrence," I replied. "We just stopped by to see how Mary was getting along ---

you know --- after the incident."

Lawrence gave us a big grin. "You absolutely wouldn't believe the changes around here."

"Changes? What changes?"

"Well, as you know, Mary has always tried to run a tight ship. If someone screws up, she'll get in their face, and most of the time the guys would go along, not because they were afraid, but because they didn't want to get evicted."

"So what's changed?"

"Now they're afraid! They're REALLY afraid. No one really believed that the old gal would use that bat of hers, but after they saw what she did to that guy, they're all believers --- every last one.

"She even left the blood on the bat as a reminder.

"The old hen is ruling the roost and has the roosters by the short hairs."

At that moment, Mary's voice came bellowing from the depths of the Three Trails.

"Feeney! Get your ass in here and clean this bathroom! I'm not going to tell you again!"

We thanked Lawrence and hurried inside.

Mary was standing at the door of bathroom number three.

"Clean those yellow stains off the wall. I just don't get it. If all you guys aimed your guns as bad as you aim your peckers, we'd all be speaking German."

That was an insight into world history that I hadn't considered before.

"Hey, Mary," I said. "It seems like you're doing OK."

Mary turned, grinned and gave us both a big hug.

"Ain't never been better.

"I'd like to chat, but I got me a crew going and if I don't stay on 'em, they slack off."

"I understand."

Just then, Feeney's head popped out the door. "We're outta butt-wipe. Can you get us another roll?"

"See what I mean," Mary said. "I'll see you guys later."

Back out on the porch two of the labor pool guys were engrossed in conversation.

I picked up on a few of their comments and we stopped to listen.

"Yea, I'm goin' over to Crystal's place tonight --- you know --- play a little hide-the-salami."

"You gonna practice safe sex, I hope?"

"Safe sex? Of course it's safe. I've hid it before, and I always found it again."

"No, fool! By safe sex, I mean you ARE gonna wear a condom, aren't you?"

"I don't know. I don't think those condoms

21

are all that safe. I had a buddy who was wearing one and got hit by a bus!"

I grabbed Maggie by her arm and hurried her off the porch.

I didn't want to take the chance that what they had was contagious.

It was still early, so we decided to just drive around for a while.

We were just passing the new shopping center in the Glover Plan district when Maggie said, "Quick, pull in there."

We drove into the parking lot and Maggie pointed to a store.

"We're going in there."

I looked where she was pointing. It was Cell Phone City.

"Why?" I asked.

"Because you need a new phone."

"There's nothing wrong with my phone. I dial a number --- it rings --- somebody answers. That's what a phone is supposed to do."

"But the new phones can do so much more,"

she protested. "They can text, take pictures, and you can even get on the Internet."

"But I don't want to text! I arrest people who are texting while they're driving."

"You have to learn how to text," she insisted. "Sometimes I just want to give you a simple message like, 'bring milk', but I'm afraid to call in case you're involved in something important.

"Now get out of the car!"

We walked in and were greeted by a twenty-something kid with a Mohawk, an earring and a lip stud.

"How can I help you?" he asked.

"We're looking for a new phone for my husband," she said.

He looked at me and grinned. "Follow me."

When we arrived at our destination, my mouth dropped open. There must have been sixty different phones to choose from.

"Are you looking for a 3G or a 4G?" he asked.

"Do you have one that comes with training wheels?"

I didn't think he got it. Kids today just don't have a sense of humor.

Seeing that I was a reluctant participant, he and Maggie engaged in a conversation about the

23

virtues of the various phones.

Finally, Maggie said, "This one is perfect."

Mr. Studley turned to me, "May I see your old phone? I can transfer all the data from your old phone to your new one."

I handed him my phone.

"Wow!" he said. "How long have you had this dinosaur?"

"I'm guessing that I bought it while you were still in grade school," I replied.

He didn't get that one either.

He hooked the phones up to a bunch of wires, pressed some buttons and in just a few minutes, the life had been sucked out of my trusty phone and transplanted into the new device.

"Watch this!" he said.

He pointed the phone at Maggie and said, "Smile."

Maggie gave him a sultry grin and he snapped her picture.

Then he handed the phone to me.

"Dial your wife's number," he instructed.

I dialed and Maggie's smiling face filled the screen.

"Now isn't that just rad?" he said.

I didn't know about 'rad', but it certainly was 'cool'.

24

"It can do all kinds of stuff," he said. "It has over 200 apps already loaded and --."

"Tell you what," I said. "Just show me how to answer the damn thing, send a text and take a picture. That's about all I can handle in one evening."

Fifteen minutes later, we left the store.

Maggie had drug me, kicking and screaming, into the phone technology of the twenty-first century.

CHAPTER 2

Arthur Manning folded the newspaper and sat back in his chair.

He had just read the obituary of his friend, Roger Beckham.

The article had read, "Roger passed away in his home after a courageous battle with cancer."

The notice was no different than the thirty-two other notices posted that day.

He had done it! He had succeeded in meeting death on his own terms.

For the first time in days, he felt a glimmer of hope as he faced his own mortality.

Two weeks ago, he had been diagnosed with ALS.

He had noticed that he was having trouble with his hands, and when the cup of hot coffee slipped from his grip, he scheduled an exam.

He had expected to be told that he had arthritis, but certainly not the dreaded Lou Gehrig's disease.

The doctor had told him that the condition was progressive and irreversible and had given him material to read.

What he had read sent chills through his body.

"The disorder causes muscle weakness and atrophy throughout the body caused by degeneration of the upper and lower motor neurons. Unable to function, the muscles weaken and atrophy. Affected individuals may ultimately lose the ability to initiate and control all voluntary movement."

Eventually, even the muscles of the rib cage atrophy, making breathing impossible. At that point a tracheostomy would be performed and he could look forward to being kept alive by mechanical ventilation.

Not if he could help it!

He had shared the news with his friend, Beckham, and in spite of the warning from Thanatos, Beckham had told him of his plan.

Now it would be his plan. It was an obvious and logical choice.

He picked up the phone and made the call.

Thanatos was angry and disappointed when he hung up the phone.

Beckham had violated a cardinal rule of the organization; he had told another patient.

He had made it clear that all referrals were to come from within the organization and that to do otherwise could jeopardize the opportunity for everyone.

Now here it was.

Manning was not a good candidate for their services because his disease was not in its advanced stages, but to deny him and risk being exposed was unacceptable.

Thanatos had encouraged Manning to wait until the disease progressed, but he was adamantly opposed.

So, reluctantly, he had agreed.

He had given Manning the usual instructions to change doctors and make the final preparations for his departure, and a date was set.

On the appointed night, Thanatos arrived at Manning's home.

Everything was in order.

Manning's condition had actually progressed faster than was usually expected and that would make his premature death more plausible.

He assembled the Thanatron machine while Manning loaded his computer disk.

After giving Manning the instructions for operating the machine and bidding him farewell, he paused by the door and watched as a beautiful array of sunsets and rainbows danced across the screen to Tchaikovsky's First Piano Concerto.

His thoughts went back to another he had known who had died of ALS after months of excruciating pain.

Finally, mercifully, his lungs had filled with pneumonia, bringing him the relief he had sought for so long.

"How," he thought as he watched Manning's peaceful face, *"could anyone think that was preferable to this?"*

An hour later, when everything had been tidied up, he took a last look at Arthur Manning.

He knew that to many, he would be considered a cold-blooded killer, but to this man, he had been an angel of mercy.

Quietly, he closed the door and vanished into the darkness.

CHAPTER 3

We had just started our morning patrol when the call came through.

Another DOA.

We arrived at the designated address and, as usual, the ambulance and another car were in the driveway.

The same EMT met us at the door. "Hey, guys," he said. "We gotta stop meeting like this. People are gonna start talking."

"Very funny," Ox said. "Who is it this time?"

"Arthur Manning. Sixty-two years old. He'd been diagnosed with ALS --- you know --- the Lou Gehrig thing.

"His daughter is in there now. Watch your step. She's a corker."

"What's that supposed to mean?" I asked.

"Lawyer --- never married --- and she's got her panties in a wad."

"About what?"

"Her old man dying. According to her, he wasn't that far gone.

"We looked around and didn't see anything that looked like foul play.

"Just giving you a heads-up."

"Swell."

A tall brunette in a crisp, no-nonsense pantsuit was standing over the body of her father.

When I extended my hand, introduced us and offered our condolences, I noticed that her eyes were not red and swollen like I was accustomed to seeing in similar situations.

"Thank you," she replied. "I'm Rhonda Manning, Arthur's only daughter."

I noticed that Manning's fingers were pinched together in an unnatural configuration.

"I understand that your father was diagnosed with ALS."

"That's true," she replied. "But that's also what makes his death so unusual."

"How do you mean?"

"People don't die of ALS. They die of complications associated with the degeneration and

31

loss of control of muscle tissue. They stop breathing because their chest muscles can't expand to fill their lungs.

"Dad just wasn't that advanced yet. He had lost some control in his hands and his lower body was starting to be affected, but nothing life threatening."

"So what are you thinking?" Ox asked.

"I don't know. Something just doesn't feel right."

"Let me take a look around the house while my partner asks you some questions."

"Who was Mr. Manning's doctor?" I asked.

She pulled an IPod from her purse and scrolled through some screens.

"Dr. Franken. Here's his number."

"Let me try to reach him," I said. "When Officer Wilson returns, we'll talk more."

I excused myself and dialed the number she had given me. After several minutes on hold, Dr. Franken came on the line.

He confirmed that Manning was his patient and that he was being treated for ALS.

He didn't seem surprised when I said that Manning had died. His response was that people react in different ways to disease and that some bodies succumb more quickly, especially if the individual had lost the will to fight.

His words were, "Often, when the individual gives up, the body does so as well."

He agreed to sign the death certificate.

I got back to Rhonda Manning just as Ox was returning from his inspection of the house.

"Ms. Manning," Ox asked, "was the door locked when you arrived this morning?"

"Yes, it was. I called, as I do every morning before going to the office. There was no answer, so I drove over. The door was locked and I let myself in with my key --- and found him like this."

"I've been all around the house," he said, "and there's no evidence of forced entry or signs of a struggle."

"I just talked with Dr. Franken," I said. "He confirmed that given your father's condition, an early death was possible. He's prepared to sign the death certificate, so we can release the body and you can make your final arrangements."

"So that's it?" she asked. "That's all you're going to do?"

"Ma'am," Ox said, "there's no sign of foul play and with the doctor signing off --- there's really not much more we can do."

"Oh, really!" she said indignantly. "Well I disagree. I want a complete autopsy, tox screen and all --- and don't call me Ma'am!"

"Yes, M --- uhh --- Ms. Manning. Let us make a call."

I went into the kitchen, dialed Captain Short and explained the situation.

"So the daughter's name is Rhonda Manning?"

"Yes. So?"

"Rhonda Manning of Manning and Fitch. They're high profile defense attorneys. "We're always knocking heads with them in the courtroom and if our prosecutor doesn't have his shit together, the guy walks.

"The last thing we want is to get into a pissing contest with them, so send Mr. Manning to the morgue and I'll authorize the autopsy."

By the time I returned and shared the news, Rhonda Manning was more composed and thanked us for our courtesy.

We instructed the EMT to transport the body to the morgue and as we were all leaving, I asked Ms. Manning, "By the way, did your father have any final instructions for his interment?"

"Why, yes. He will be cremated. Why do you ask?"

"Just curious." I said.

34

Two days later, the captain called Ox and me into his office.

"Well, it appears that Rhonda Manning may have been right.

"The initial examination of the body found nothing but a needle mark on the arm, which is consistent for a man undergoing medical treatment."

"I'm guessing that the tox screen showed something else," I said.

"Exactly. Four ingredients were found in Manning's bloodstream; a simple saline solution, sodium thiopental which is a sleep inducing barbiturate, pancuronium bromide which is a muscle relaxant and potassium chloride which will stop the heart."

"So Manning was poisoned?" Ox asked.

"Yes and no," the captain replied. "These chemicals were no doubt the cause of death, but they are also the signature chemicals used in euthanasia.

"Manning most likely administered the dosage to himself --- with someone's help."

"So you think we're dealing with a new Dr. Death?" I asked.

"Who's Dr. Death?" Ox asked.

"Dr. Jack Kevorkian," the captain said. "He was a pathologist who was best known for championing a terminal patient's right-to-die by physician assisted suicide.

"Between 1990 and 1998, he allegedly assisted in the deaths of one hundred and thirty terminally ill patients."

"Didn't he die in prison?" I asked.

"No. In 1999, he was convicted of second-degree murder and served eight years of a ten-to twenty-five year sentence. In 2007, he was paroled and died four years later."

"But his legacy lives on, doesn't it?" I asked.

"Indeed it does. Euthanasia is still a very hot topic.

"The majority of Americans are firmly against it --- mostly on religious grounds, but there are thousands who champion the death-with-dignity concept and organizations abound that are fighting for the right to control their own destiny.

"One of the original groups was called the Hemlock Society, but it evolved into a group called Compassion & Choices. Then there's the Death With Dignity National Center and several others."

"So is euthanasia illegal or not?" Ox asked.

"It's legal in only three states, Oregon,

Washington and Montana, but there are severe restrictions even there.

"And that brings us to our current situation. It's definitely against the law in Missouri and it would appear that someone out there is helping terminal patients die."

"Doesn't this fall into the 'victimless crime' category?" I asked. "Kind of like prostitution?"

"That's not really the point, is it, Walt? If it's illegal, it's illegal. We may or may not agree, but it's our job to enforce the law. We arrest johns and hookers all the time. This is no different.

"Besides, do you want to be the one to tell Rhonda Manning that someone helped pump the suicide cocktail into her dad and we're going to look the other way?"

"I see what you mean. Sorry!"

"You and Ox brought this thing in, so I'm going to have the two of you look into it.

"There's one organization that's a bit more aggressive in assisting patients. It's called the Final Exit Network. I'm thinking they, or an offshoot of the group, may have formed in the Kansas City area.

"It's going to involve a lot of grunt work, but it has to be done."

"So what's our assignment?" Ox asked.

"I want you to go back through the records for

the past twelve months and take a close look at all of the non-violent deaths where a doctor signed off on the death certificate. See if you can find a pattern."

"But that's hundreds!" I said.

"Then you'd better get busy!"

I learned in my real estate career that the only way to succeed was to develop a system to organize your work.

The task of reviewing the hundreds of files seemed almost impossible at first, but finally we settled on a procedure that made some sense.

Ox would pull a file and check for cause of death and see who signed off.

Only the files where the death was non-violent and where a physician signed off were given to me.

I created a matrix where I could record age, cause of death and the name of the doctor.

In the beginning, I could see no pattern whatsoever.

I soon discovered that there were almost three thousand doctors in the Kansas City metropolitan area, and any one of them could have signed the

38

death certificate.

After several hundred entries, I began to see a pattern emerge.

When the age was seventy or over, and the cause of death was some type of terminal illness, like cancer, four physicians had significantly more entries than any other; Dr. Benjamin Stein, Dr. Stanley Goebel, Dr. Israel Franken and Dr. Roland Graves.

BINGO!

I showed the data to Ox and we decided to take our investigation one step further before we reported to the captain.

The next of kin was listed on each report and we randomly picked a half-dozen files to call.

We told them that we were simply following up, but the one question we asked every time was, "How was your loved one interred?"

Without exception, the answer was "cremation".

How convenient!

There were no bodies to exhume and test for deadly chemicals. They had been burned to ashes.

We were anxious to report our findings to the captain.

Our data indicated that a new Dr. Death was alive and well in Kansas City.

CHAPTER 4

When I arrived at my building that evening, it was obvious that someone had convened a meeting on the front porch.

My building used to be a six-plex.

When Maggie and I were married, I converted the two top floor apartments to one large unit big enough for both of us.

My dad, who only recently re-entered my life, and my old college philosophy professor live in the bottom two units.

Bernice, Dad's new squeeze, and a goofy guy we call Jerry The Joker live in the second floor units.

My old friend and maintenance man, Willie, lives in a kitchenette in the basement.

All of them were standing there watching me come up the sidewalk.

Dad spoke first.

"How about helping your old man and Bernice become a king and queen?"

"Excuse me?"

"King and queen --- at the Senior's Ball --- we need sponsors."

Sensing that I was still confused, the Professor chimed in.

"The Lakeside Assisted Living Center is sponsoring a fund raiser.

"Tomorrow night they're having a Senior's Ball. There will be a band and at the end of the evening. Any couple seventy and over, can participate in a dance-a-thon."

"Yea," Dad said. "It's like a walk-a-thon, only we'll be dancing. The couple that dances the longest gets to be the king and queen of the ball.

"That's gonna be us. Right, Sweetie?"

Bernice giggled and nodded her head.

"So what's the sponsor part?" I asked.

"Every couple that dances, gets people to sponsor them," Dad said. "You pledge money for every minute that your couple stays on the floor."

"We're all going," Jerry said.

"Well, are you in, kid?" Dad asked expectantly.

How could I refuse?

41

"I'll ask Maggie. If it's OK with her, I'm in for a buck a minute."

"Then it's settled," Dad said. "Maggie's already on board."

I should have known.

"Better include Mary," I said as I entered the building. "You know how she loves to dance."

"Already done!" came the reply.

Maggie met me at the door with a big hug and kiss.

"Looks like we're going to be dancing with the oldies tomorrow night," I said.

"It'll be fun. We haven't been dancing for weeks. I haven't seen Bernice and your Dad so excited since the day they were arrested on top of the WWI Memorial."

"Don't remind me, please!"

I noticed that Maggie had set the table with our best dishes and the light from two long tapered candles reflected in the crystal glasses filled with Arbor Mist, Peach Chardonnay, my favorite.

A steaming tuna casserole, another personal

favorite, sat on a hot pad in front of my plate.

I was beginning to think that maybe Maggie had some hanky-panky on her mind.

I was thoroughly enjoying the lovely meal that Maggie had prepared, but I couldn't get the images of Roger Beckham and Arthur Manning out of my head.

Maggie sensed my preoccupation.

"What's on your mind, Walt?"

"Euthanasia. You know --- death with dignity --- how do you feel about that?"

"Well, I know you sure know how to kill a mood!"

"No. I'm serious. Have you ever thought about that?"

I proceeded to tell her about Beckham and Manning and about the results of the investigation that Ox and I had done.

"It looks like a new Dr. Death is out there helping terminally ill patients end their suffering and I'm supposed to help catch the guy. I just don't know how I feel about it. That's all."

"Well, you know I was raised as a good Catholic girl and graduated from a Catholic school. I remember the nuns saying that suicide was a mortal sin, along with a lot of other stuff."

"I didn't ask you what the nuns thought. I

asked you what you think."

"You really are serious, aren't you?

"Actually, I've never quite fit the mold of a devout Catholic, and I've never really given the subject much thought, so let's just say that I'm open minded."

"I'm going to share something with you that I've never told anyone else."

Maggie gave me her full attention.

"When I was in high school, we had an old dog. Her name was Sugar.

"We had her a long time and eventually, she became ill. She had trouble walking. She kept bumping into furniture. She lost control of her bladder and left little dribbles all over the house and worst of all she would whimper; the most pitiful cry you have ever heard."

"It must have been difficult to watch," Maggie said.

"It was. One day, Dad was on the road and Mom had to go to work, so she asked me to drive Sugar to the vet.

"The vet examined her and then told me there was nothing he could do for her. He said that the humane thing would be to put her to sleep.

"I asked if I could be with her and he said that I could.

"I remember there were two chairs side-by-side. Sugar was in one chair and I was in the other.

"She looked into my eyes and laid her head in my lap. I stroked her head as the doctor gave her the injection.

"Her eyes slowly closed and she was gone --- forever --- just like that."

"Walt, I'm so sorry."

"On the way home, my eyes were so full of tears, I had to pull to the side of the road. I cried harder that day than ever in my life."

Maggie reached over and held my hand.

"You know how much I like Elvis?"

"Yes."

"Elvis has a beautiful song titled, "Old Shep."

"To this day, I still can't bring myself to listen to the song.

"When I hear the words,

"As the years fast did roll, Old Shep, he grew old.

"His eyes were fast growing dim.

"And one day the doctor looked at me and said, "I can't do no more for him, Jim." I remember that day just like it was yesterday."

A tear rolled down my cheek.

"You know that's why I love you, you big galoot."

"Because I'm a crybaby?"

"No, because you can be Mr. Macho man when you have to be, but inside, where it counts, you're a loving, caring human being."

"OK," I said, wiping the tears away. "What I can't get my head around is why it's humane to end an animal's suffering, and not a man's. It seems to me that, once again, Lady Justice has her head up her ass."

"So what are you going to do?" she asked.

"I guess it's like the captain said, 'It's illegal in Missouri.'

"I'm a cop and I've sworn to uphold the law, so I guess I really don't have a choice."

"Well, you have a choice right now," she said, pulling me to my feet. "You can stay in here and feel sorry for yourself or you can come with me.

"I think I might have something that will take your mind off all this morbid stuff."

I followed and, sure enough, she was right!

When she had finished taking my mind off the morbid stuff, she slipped out of bed and went to the bathroom.

While she was away, I picked up my new cell phone from the nightstand.

She came back into the room and was about to put on her nightie when I pressed the button and the room lit up with the flash.

A horrified look came on her face.

"Walter Williams! You erase that right now!"

She used my full name, so I figured I had better comply.

"Yes, Ma'am."

CHAPTER 5

Promptly at six o'clock, all the expectant revelers were gathered on the front step.

A quick glance told me that we would have to take two cars.

Dad, Bernice and the Professor piled in with Maggie; Willie, Mary and Jerry hopped in with me.

I should have known that it was a mistake to take Jerry.

He's seventy-three years old, looks like Mr. Peepers and fancies himself the Kansas City version of Rodney Dangerfield.

He almost drove us nuts with his incessant jokes, until we turned him on to the 'open mike' night at the Comedy Club.

Now, we occasionally get to be guinea pigs for some of his new material.

We were barely to the first intersection when he started.

"Walt! I'm adding a new dimension to my nightclub act --- limericks! Would you like to hear one?"

"Do I have a choice?"

He ignored my snide remark and plunged ahead.

"There once was a fellow, McSweeney
  Who spilled some gin on his weenie.
  Just to be couth
  He added vermouth
  And slipped his girlfriend a martini."

"I don't get it," Mary said.
Undaunted, Jerry continued.

"There once was a man from Nantucket."

"Stop right there!" I said. "Off color is OK, but no vulgarity!"

"I'm offended!" Jerry said with a woebegone look on his face.

"I don't do vulgar; I do funny. Just listen."

49

"There once was a man from Nantucket
Who kept all his cash in a bucket.
But his daughter named Nan
Ran away with a man.
And as for the bucket, Nan Tucket."

"See!" he said.

"I apologize."

Thankfully, by that time, we were pulling into the parking lot of the Lakeside Assisted Living Center.

I was immediately impressed.

The complex was situated on about ten acres. In front of the building was a large lake, complete with geese and walking trails.

We piled out of the cars and entered the spacious lobby.

A matronly lady with her hair pulled back in a bun, greeted us.

"Good evening. My name is Lucille Baldwin and I'll be your hostess for the tour."

I grabbed Dad by the arm.

"Tour! What tour? You didn't say anything about a tour."

"Calm down, Sonny. Lakeside is sponsoring the Senior's Ball for two reasons: to raise money for Alzheimer's research and to introduce people to their facility.

"It's no big deal. Probably take fifteen minutes --- tops."

"Swell!"

Lucille led us through a door and into a corridor on the left.

"This is the assisted living wing. It has been designed for people who are still in relatively good health and can care for themselves.

"We provide services such as room cleaning, laundry and meals.

"This room belongs to Mr. and Mrs. Lathrop. They've been kind enough to share it with us this evening."

I peeked into the room and was amazed to see a spacious area containing two twin beds, two recliner chairs, a big screen TV, a small table with two wooden chairs, a small fridge, a microwave and a good size closet.

Mrs. Lathrop invited us in.

"We've been here two years and absolutely love it! Lakeside has everything we need."

I wondered how much they were paying her for that spiel.

A bit farther down the hall, I decided that she probably was telling the truth.

"This is the library," Lucille said, "and this is

the game and activity room.

"We have all kinds of activities for the residents; bingo, bridge, bible study.

"Every Thursday, a local winery sponsors a wine and cheese party for those who are interested."

Mary pulled me aside and whispered in my ear.

"Walt. What do you think about having one of them wine and cheese things at the hotel? You know how I love cheese."

I could just picture my band of misfits swirling the wine in crystal glasses and sniffing the bouquet.

The thought brought to mind the day that Ox and I rousted a couple of drunks from an alley in downtown KC.

They were propped up against the alley wall on a couple of old crates, passing a gallon bottle back and forth.

Each time the bottle was passed, they would shout a chorus together.

"What's the word? Thunderbird!
"What's the price? Sixty twice!"

"What in the world are they talking about?" I asked Ox.

"Thunderbird," Ox replied, "is the drink of choice for our local winos, and it only costs a dollar and twenty cents for a gallon --- sixty twice --- get it?"

So I learned that day that it was possible to duck into an alley and drink yourself into oblivion for a buck twenty.

I whispered back to Mary, "Unless it was Thunderbird, I doubt our guys would be interested."

"What are you talkin' about?"

"Never mind. I just don't think it would be a very good idea. How about I just bring you some cheese?"

"That'll work," she said, grinning.

On the way back to the lobby, Maggie grabbed my arm.

"Walt! This place is fantastic. I could live here --- you know --- when the time comes."

Dad overheard her remark.

"If you want to live here someday, Sweetie, you'd better be saving some dollars. Four grand --- a month --- each!"

"Wow!" I thought. *"You could buy a lot of wine and cheese for four grand!"*

Maggie whispered again, "Never mind."

Lucille led us back into the big entry way and through the door into the opposite wing.

"This is the acute care wing," she said, holding the door for us. "Once a resident's health deteriorates to the point where they can no longer care for themselves, they are transferred here."

I stepped through the door and into another world.

If the wing we were just in seemed like a little bit of heaven, then the lobby must have been purgatory, because I felt like I had just entered hell.

I looked around and instead of seeing smiling people on their way to bingo or bridge, I saw a row of wheelchairs along the corridor.

Some of the occupants were tied in to keep them upright; others slumped to the side. All of them were slack-jawed with sunken faces. Dark eyes stared vacantly into the distance.

As we moved down the hall, I could look into the rooms and see residents in their beds with oxygen tubes attached to their noses and catheter bags attached to the bedside.

It was obvious that Lakeside was doing its best. There was the aroma of an antiseptic deodorant, but it just couldn't mask the smell of decay, desperation and death.

As we passed between the wheelchair-bound residents, my eyes locked with those of an old woman.

She raised her hands toward me and her lips parted, but there was no sound.

She didn't have to speak. Her eyes said it all. *"HELP ME!"*

No one spoke during our tour of the acute wing. I could only imagine the thoughts going through the minds of my elderly friends.

In my own mind, I was seeing the old woman in the wheelchair and then seeing the peaceful body of Arthur Manning.

What was happening to the old woman was acceptable, but the person who had assisted Arthur Manning was wanted for murder.

It just didn't seem right.

Thankfully, the tour ended and Lucille led us to the gymnasium where the Senior's Ball was to be held.

When we entered the gym, I felt like I had stepped back fifty years to my senior prom.

There were balloons, crepe paper streamers and table decorations.

55

There was a table full of all kinds of good things to eat and an open bar.

Mary spied little cubes of cheese, which brightened her mood immediately.

The dance was to start at promptly seven p.m., and at five minutes before the hour, the band arrived.

It was the Ed Smith Trio.

Maggie and I had danced to Ed's music several times before.

Ed had been a fixture at senior's dances for many years. He had played at Senior Centers, Legion Halls, Shrine Dances and in church basements.

All the old folks loved him because he played the music of their lives --- mostly from the thirties and forties with a little fifties mixed in.

It was music you could really dance to and these old folks knew how to dance.

The band consisted of Ed on the tenor sax, a lady on keyboard and another old guy on drums. All together, they were probably two hundred and fifty years old --- but they could really belt it out.

Throughout the evening, we did the foxtrot to *Cab Driver* and *New York, New York*. We twirled to the *Tennessee Waltz*. We did the cha-cha to *Cherry Pink And Apple Blossom White* and the west coast swing to *Honky-Tonk*.

56

Halfway through the dance, Ed announced, "OK everybody! It's time for a fuuuuun mixer!"

About two-thirds of the dancers left their chairs. The guys lined up on one side of the room and the ladies on the other.

These were the singles, seniors without partners. At this age, those whose partners had passed on far exceeded those who were still together.

I took Maggie's hand and held it tight.

I had been alone for many years, but now that she was in my life, I don't know what I would do without her.

The couples paired up and danced until Ed blew the whistle at which time they changed partners.

I knew for sure I never wanted to change partners again.

The dance-a-thon was scheduled for nine o'clock.

Dad, Bernice and the other contestants gathered on the floor.

The rules were that Ed would play continuously until the last couple was left standing.

Lots of dancers started the contest, but at seventy and older, the crowd had dwindled after a half hour.

An hour into the dance, only three couples remained.

When it was all over, Dad and Bernice proudly donned the crowns as king and queen.

It had been a good evening.

I was a proud son and it only cost me eighty-seven dollars.

CHAPTER 6

It had been several days since Ox and I submitted our Dr. Death data to the captain.

Every morning, I expected him to call us in his office and share the news that our hard work had produced some valuable leads, but days passed and the call never came.

We had resumed our regular patrol and our shift was filled with the usual traffic stops, domestic disturbance calls and the occasional flasher.

It wasn't glamorous, but it was the job, and frankly, after my latest near-death experience, I welcomed the break.

Maggie and I were in our jammies and were about to settle in for an evening of TV when there was a knock on the door.

I opened the door and found myself staring into the solemn faces of my five tenants.

My first thought was that one of them had organized a protest group against the landlord, but I didn't remember hearing any recent grumbling.

Dad spoke first. "Hey, Sonny. Can we come in?"

I looked at Maggie who had slipped on a robe. She just shrugged her shoulders.

"Uhhh --- sure. Come on in."

We hustled up some chairs and sat in a circle like Indians having a pow-wow.

"OK," I said. "To what do we owe the pleasure of this visit?"

"We wanted to talk to you about these," Dad said, handing me a stack of papers.

"What are they?"

"These are our Advance Health Care Directives," Dad said. "We were all really bummed out after touring the acute care facility the other night.

"And after the scare that Bernice gave us --- well --- none of us wanted to wind up like those poor folks in the wheelchairs, so we decided we should do something about it."

A couple of months ago, Bernice had passed out in her apartment and was rushed to the hospital.

Thankfully, it was nothing serious, but it certainly was a reality check for us all.

"Where did you come up with these? Did you hire an attorney?"

"Heck, no," Jerry said. "We made a visit to the Three Trails. Mary's pretty tight with that Wingate fellow --- you know --- the computer geek.

"He had a program on his laptop called "Family Lawyer". He printed them out for us."

"Oh great!" I thought. *"End-of-life legal decisions coming from the Three Trails Hotel. What could possibly go wrong with that?"*

I looked at the documents and noted that all of them had designated me as the agent to make their health-care decisions.

Then I read the box that all of them had checked.

"I do not want my life to be prolonged, nor do I wish to be provided artificial hydration or nutrition if (i) I have an incurable and irreversible condition that will result in my death within a relatively short time, (ii) I become unconscious and, to a reasonable degree of medical certainty, I will not regain consciousness, or (iii) the likely risks and burdens of treatment would outweigh the expected benefits."

I stared at the document in disbelief.

"I can't do this!" I said. "I couldn't 'pull the

plug' on people I love! Who am I to make life and death decisions?"

"But we don't want to be vegetables!" Bernice said with conviction.

Jerry, of course, couldn't let that one pass.

"If you were a vegetable, have you ever thought about what you would be?

"Pastor Bob, for instance. He would be lettuce because he's always saying, "Lettuce pray."

"I got one!" Dad said. "Bernice is one hot tomato."

Bernice giggled and punched him in the arm.

"Then the Professor chimed in. "That's not exactly correct. Technically, the tomato is classified as a fruit."

"That works too," Jerry said. "Take Willie there. If he were a fruit he'd be a blackberry. BLACK-berry. Get it?"

"An' if you keep dat up, funny man," Willie retorted, "you gonna be a SQUASH!"

I couldn't believe how quickly the conversation had deteriorated.

"Let's get back to the question at hand," I said. "Have you all really thought this through?

"By signing these documents, you are agreeing to end your life. It's like a suicide pact."

"Well, not really," Dad said. "To me, suicide

is when you take your own life. In this case you're going to do it for us."

"Oh, now I feel a whole lot better. Instead of you committing suicide, I get to be a murderer."

"Yea," Jerry said, "that suicide thing can be pretty tricky.

"I heard about an old lady who had an incurable disease. She decided to end it all by shooting herself through the heart. Not wanting to make a mistake, she phoned her doctor and asked him the exact location of her heart.

"He told her that the heart was located exactly two inches below the left nipple.

"The old woman hung up the phone, took careful aim and shot herself in the left knee."

"You're a jerk!" Bernice retorted.

"Seriously, Walt," the Professor said, "these Health-Care Directives and Do-Not Resuscitate instructions are standard forms and quite commonly used.

"It's a 'quality-of-life' decision. Think of your own situation. If you were bedridden and unconscious and the only thing keeping you alive were tubes and respirators, would you want to live like that?"

I had to admit that I wouldn't.

"Actually," the Professor said, "the ideal way

to go would be like the opening scene in *Soylent Green*."

"Wot's soylent green?" Willie asked.

"*Soylent Green* was the 1973 sci-fi movie staring Charlton Heston.

"The setting was a futuristic society that permitted people to make end-of-life decisions on their own terms.

"I loved the scene where an old man was being taken into a beautiful room. He was relaxed in a comfortable bed in front of a huge movie screen. Pictures of mountain ranges, sunsets, rainbows and beaches played on the panoramic screen while soft, comforting music filled the air.

"When it was time, a sedative was administered and then the drug that peacefully put him to sleep."

My mind filled with images of Roger Beckham and Arthur Manning.

"It sounds beautiful," Dad said. "What was so 'sci-fi' about it?"

"It's what they did with the body after he was gone," the Professor said. "There was a food shortage and bodies of the deceased were ground up to make food --- hence, the *Soylent Green*."

"I guess there's more than one way to become a vegetable." Jerry said.

"You're just gross!" Bernice said, wrinkling her nose.

I looked at the documents again.

There was another paragraph that authorized the harvesting of organs of the deceased.

I mentioned that everyone had checked the 'yes' box except Willie.

"By de time I go, ain't nobody gonna want none o' my parts 'cause I will have done worn 'em out --- all except one, of course --- an' I don't think dey do no transplants wit dat thing."

"From what I hear," Dad said, "that 'thing' ought to be donated to a museum somewhere. It's a legend."

"Or maybe you could will it to Emma," Bernice said. "She might want it as a keepsake."

I could tell by the look on Willie's face that he was proud to be the stuff of legends.

"I've never been an organ donor before," Jerry said, "but I once gave an old piano to the Salvation Army."

I could see that our discussion was going nowhere, so I suggested that we call it an evening.

"I'll hang on to these for you," I said. "If any of you have second thoughts, please let me know."

When everyone was gone, I turned to Maggie.

"So what's your take on all that?" I asked.

65

"Actually, I've thought about it myself. I know lots of people who have DNR's and Living Wills.

"When I was single, I really didn't have anyone to make those decisions for me, but now that I have you --- maybe we should consider it."

"I get what everyone is saying. In those circumstances, it would make sense not to prolong the inevitable, but there's a problem I'm struggling with.

"Let's look at this again."

I reread the health care directive.

"What this is saying is that if I have an incurable disease that will lead to my death, I don't want to live and I'm giving the designated agent the authority to end my life.

"HOW IS THIS DIFFERENT FROM WHAT DR. DEATH IS DOING?"

Maggie just shrugged her shoulders.

"If I pull the plug on Dad or Bernice, I'm just an agent doing my job, but Dr. Death is a murderer.

"I don't get it. There's no justice here!"

"I wish I could help you, Walt, but I don't understand the distinction either."

I knew I wouldn't sleep and misery loves company, so I decided to give Pastor Bob a call.

While I'm not a card-carrying member of any church, Pastor Bob is my designated clergyman.

I met him several years ago.

He had just walked away from a huge mainline Protestant Church because they were pressuring him to preach their political agenda from the pulpit.

When he left, more than half of the congregation followed him.

On the day he walked into my real estate office, he was a shepherd with a flock, but no church building.

I found him a home in an abandoned chapel on Linwood Boulevard and he and his followers have prospered.

What he didn't realize at the time was that he was going to inherit a goofy old ex-realtor who wanted to be a cop.

On more than one occasion, my escapades in law enforcement have left me broken, depressed and doubting.

It was Pastor Bob who helped pull me through those trying times.

I made the call.

"Good evening," came the voice. "This is dial-a-prayer. For a mere thirty pieces of silver, your supplications will be forwarded to the Almighty."

"Oh, sorry. I must have the wrong number."

"Relax, Walt. This is Pastor Bob. I saw your name on the caller ID and thought I'd give you a hard time."

"Are you like this with all your parishioners?"

"No, I make an exception for you."

"I know it's late ---."

"Walt, it always is late when you call. I wouldn't expect anything different. Come on over."

Pastor Bob met me at the sanctuary door and led me into his office.

"So what is the current moral dilemma upon whose horns you are currently impaled?"

"How long did it take you to put that together?" I asked.

"Oh, I worked it up while you were driving over here. Pretty clever, don't you think?"

"Well, I actually do have something I'm struggling with."

"Walt, you're like the little boy who's constantly asking his daddy questions like, 'Where does air come from?' or 'How long is forever?'

"What's today's topic?"

"Euthanasia."

"Ahhh, yes. And you've come here expecting me to tell you whether it's right or wrong, a sin or not a sin. Am I right?"

"Well, sort of. I'm interested in your perspective from a religious standpoint."

"I wish it were that easy.

"Many people, especially people of fundamentalist faiths have a strict interpretation of right and wrong. It's either black or it's white.

"My position, however, is that life is not that clear-cut. There is some black and some white, but there are also a million shades of gray in between."

"I did some reading on the subject," I said, "and it seems that virtually every mainstream religion of the world, from Christianity to Judaism to Islam all condemn euthanasia."

"That's true. It is based in the idea that one's life is the property of God and a gift to the world and to destroy that life is to wrongly assert dominion over what is God's."

"So it's OK for any guy with a dick to create life and bring it into the world with impunity, but to bring it to an end when all hope is gone is murder."

"It is an interesting dichotomy, isn't it?"

"I suppose 'Thou shalt not kill' is also involved."

"It is, but it's a very weak argument. There are so many shades of gray there that it's ridiculous --- even in the Bible."

"How so?"

"You quoted a scripture from the Ten Commandments. There are dozens of others that are used to condemn killing of any kind.

"In fact, the Bible is full of stories of people smiting one another in the name of the Lord.

"Take David. He slays Goliath and becomes the leader of an army that slays thousands --- and that's all OK.

"Later, he sends Uriah the Hittite into battle knowing he will be killed because he wants to do the nasty with Uriah's wife, Bathsheba."

"I'm guessing that didn't go over too well with the Big Guy?"

" No, it didn't. But that's not the point.

"In both instances, it was the same act ---

killing --- but it was the circumstances that dictated whether it was right or wrong.

"We have been sending our young men and women into battle since the beginning of time. Their task is to kill the enemy and we welcome them home as heroes.

"Islam is very outspoken condemning suicide, and every week we hear of Muslims blowing up restaurants with bombs strapped to their bodies --- The Jihad, or Holy War.

"Let's bring it a little closer to home," he said. "If I remember correctly, Mary Murphy bashed in the skull of a man that was about to waste you and Maggie.

"Sin or no sin? You tell me.

"What man, if faced with the decision of taking a life, would not pull the trigger if it meant saving a loved one?

"Sin or no sin? You tell me."

"You're preaching to the choir," I replied. "I totally understand that circumstances can alter truths, but if that's the case, why is there so much opposition to euthanasia? It's legal in only three states."

"Besides the religious component," he replied, "the biggest argument against euthanasia is the 'slippery slope'."

"What in the world is that?"

"It's the notion that if euthanasia becomes widely accepted, it will lead to abuse. It will be used for purposes other than those for which it was intended."

"Such as?"

"Such as a greedy child prematurely putting away an ailing parent to speed up an inheritance or a spouse putting his partner down because he or she has found greener pastures --- remember David and Bathsheba?"

I was about to protest when I remembered how Lawrence Wingate's wife got power-of-attorney and cleaned out poor Lawrence while he was getting a heart by-pass.

"And then there's the folks who aren't dying, but are so deep in depression that they wish they could. There are certainly a lot of possibilities for abuse of the system."

"But that argument has holes too," I said. "It's like the old saying, 'Guns don't kill people. People kill people'."

I was getting fired up. "Automobiles kill more people every year than almost anything else. Yet, we still have guns and we still have cars and we have laws that punish people who don't use them properly.

"If we can do that with guns and cars, why not euthanasia?"

He just shrugged, "You tell me.

"Things evolve over time. Ninety years ago, alcohol was illegal and prohibition was the law.

"The fact that it is not against the law now doesn't excuse the moon shiners and gin runners back then."

"But it's just not fair," I protested.

"Maybe one day it will be legal, but right now, it is what it is.

"Walt, if you will recall, the last time we had one of these little chats, we talked about free will."

"Yes, I remember."

"We all have choices to make every day.

"It would be so much easier if there were iron-clad rules that told you what choices to make in every situation, but there just aren't.

"We have been given guidelines as to what is right and what is wrong, but circumstances alter cases, and all we can do is make the best choice possible at the time."

I sensed that I had gotten as much from the reverend as I was going to get, so I thanked him and said my farewells.

On the way home, I realized that, once again, I had gone to Pastor Bob looking for a definite 'yes or no' and left with a 'maybe'.

It seemed that every time when it was all said

and done, the answers I had been seeking were not in a book or written as a commandment, but were to be found somewhere deep inside myself.

Pastor Bob has a way of making you look there.

Maybe that's why I like him.

CHAPTER 7

The next morning, Ox and I were summoned into the captain's office.

"At last," I thought, *"maybe our data mining had paid some dividends."*

The captain's first words took the wind right out of my sails.

"We've come to a dead-end on this Dr. Death thing."

He must have seen the expression on my face.

"It's not your fault, Walt. You and Ox did a fantastic job and your data pointed us in the right direction, but these guys simply covered their tracks too well."

"What about the four doctors that had the high clusters of deaths?" I asked.

"Since all the bodies had been cremated, there was really no forensic evidence that could link any of the doctors to the euthanasia thing. From a statistical point of view, those clusters could have happened by chance. Any good defense attorney would have a field day."

"But what about Arthur Manning?" Ox asked. "We had forensic evidence there."

"Indeed we did. Manning was Dr. Franken's patient.

"We made some discreet inquiries because we didn't want to tip anyone off that we had suspicions, and it seems that Dr. Franken was in Palm Beach, Florida attending a medical conference on the night Manning was --- uhhh --- euthanized."

"How convenient," I said.

"Yes, isn't it?" he replied. "It seems that what we have is a group of physicians associated with some version of this Final Exit Network. Apparently, they refer patients whom they feel are qualified for their services, to an individual who actually assists the patients with the final steps.

"Since they are not directly associated with the act itself, they can create alibis and insulate themselves from our investigation."

"So there really is a 'Dr. Death' out there doing the deed!" I said.

"That's our theory," he replied, "and it looks like the only way to get to him is through one of the doctors, but there is one more avenue that I want you to explore, the chemicals he uses in his death cocktail.

"Potassium chloride of the strength and purity he needs, isn't something you can just go buy at the local pharmacy and it's not something one of the doctors would normally have laying around his office.

"This guy has to be getting it from somewhere. Find out where you can buy the stuff locally and see if you can find a connection.

"Will do!"

It was back to the Internet to learn more about the uses of potassium chloride and where it could be purchased.

We found that its primary use was as an ingredient in fertilizer, but I was surprised to discover that this chemical that could stop a heart was also used in water treatments. It was also a component of the Ice Melt used on sidewalks.

There were four companies in the Kansas City area that were suppliers of the chemical.

"So what are we going to do?" Ox asked. "Just march in and ask some guy if he's selling the stuff to Dr. Death?"

"We could ask for a list of all his sales of potassium chloride, but I'd be willing to bet that even if he was, it would be off the books."

"I have a thought," Ox said. "Let's cross-check the owners of the companies with the list of deaths we ran for the last twelve months.

"It's a long shot, but if one of our suspicious deaths ties in with one of the companies, it could be a lead."

We spent the afternoon pouring over our database and discovered that the wife of Warren Flynn, the owner of West Side Chemicals, had died of complications of multiple sclerosis.

Her physician was Dr. Stein and, of course, she had been cremated.

"That's way too much coincidence," I said. "This has to be our guy!"

West Side Chemicals was on Mulberry Street in the West Bottoms.

The business was in an old brick structure that had a rail spur leading to a loading dock.

"How do you want to handle this?" Ox asked.

"No point beating around the bush," I replied. "Let's just hit him right between the eyes and watch his reaction."

A man in his late fifties rose from his desk when we entered.

"May I help you?"

"Are you Warren Flynn?"

"Yes."

"I'm Officer Williams and this is my partner, Officer Wilson. We'd like to ask you a few questions."

"Sure. How can I help?"

"There's no delicate way to say this Mr. Flynn.

"I'm so sorry to hear about your wife. I know it can't be easy watching someone you love waste away.

"No one would blame you for wanting to help end her suffering and leave this world with some dignity."

"What are you saying? That I killed my wife!"

"Absolutely not! But we were wondering if she might have had some help ending it herself."

"I have absolutely no idea what you're talking about."

"Oh, I think you do. We believe that Dr. Stein

79

referred you to someone associated with a euthanasia society like the Final Exit Group.

"We also believe that you might be supplying this someone with the potassium chloride he needs to do his work."

"I have nothing to hide and nothing to apologize for. You can look at my books anytime you want. You don't even need a warrant."

"I really didn't think that we'd find anything there. We were hoping that you would be willing to cooperate with us."

"I have tremendous respect for what you do," he said, "but it seems to me that the police department's resources could be better spent looking for the crack heads, rapists and muggers that roam our city streets. I'm sorry. I can't help you."

I wanted to say that I disagreed with him, but I couldn't.

We reported back to the captain that the chemical lead was a dead end.

"I was afraid of that," he said, "so we may have to go after Dr. Death from a different angle."

"Any ideas on how to do that?" Ox asked.

"Well actually, we do have an idea," he said, looking squarely at me.

"What?"

Then it hit me.

"No! Not again!"

"Walt, you seem to be our 'go-to' guy lately for undercover work, and this one is right up your alley."

"How do you figure that?"

"We need someone to pose as a terminally ill patient and you're the closest thing to dead that we have."

I couldn't believe he had said that.

In my three years on the force, I had been undercover as half of a gay couple with Vince.

I had been a 'john' in a prostitution sting because I looked 'needy', and most recently I had dyed and slicked back my hair to impersonate a thug.

I had even donned a dress and a wig to pose as a transvestite, supposedly because I had the best-looking legs.

But now, to inherit this job because they figured I was on death's door was one distinction I didn't appreciate.

"Do you really think I'm that far gone?" I asked.

"Not really, he replied with a smile, "but we have people who can make you look like you are."

"I suppose that means more make-up?"

I looked over at Ox who was doing his best to suppress a giggle.

I remembered him actually laughing out loud when he caught me in my bra and panties.

"Maybe one day they'll need a fat guy and it'll be your turn," I said.

He gave me one of those 'now you've hurt my feelings' looks.

"The last time I checked," I said, "I was in fairly decent health. How are you going to get around that?"

"It's all been taken care of," the captain said, handing me a folder. "Meet Ray Braxton, the new you."

"So who is Ray Braxton?" I asked, opening the folder.

"Not 'is', but 'was'," he replied. "Ray died in prison. He was eaten up with cancer on the inside. He had no family, so when he passed, as far as the world was concerned, Ray Braxton didn't exist.

"We have his complete medical record from the prison including x-rays, blood work --- everything."

"But won't the doctor want to do tests of his

82

own?"

"Not after he sees Braxton's records. He would see it as a waste of time and money."

"So which doctor is the target?"

"Dr. Graves. You will have gotten his name from Roger Beckham."

"All the patients died in their homes. How are we going to handle that?"

"We'll use one of our safe houses. It's all set up; just like home."

"Seems like you've thought of everything," I said. "What's our timetable?"

"How about right now? Our makeup artist is waiting for you."

"Oh really! How did you know I would I would even go along with this hair-brained scheme?"

"You've never let me down yet."

The captain introduced me to a young lady named Samantha.

She looked like Betty Rizzo, the beauty school dropout from the movie, *Grease*.

"Call me Sam," she said, sticking out her paw.

"Hi. I'm Walt. Is this going to hurt?"

She grinned and popped her gum. "Naw, I'll be gentle, but it is going to take awhile, so just sit back, relax and let me make you look like a dead man."

"Swell!"

As we progressed, she gave me a running narrative of what she was doing.

"It starts with the skin. You've got some wrinkles --- that's good --- we'll just enhance them to give you a more shriveled look.

"Next is the color. You need to be real pale and that's gonna take a lot of foundation."

She started spreading gunk on my face with a wooden spatula. I felt like a piece of bread being buttered for the grill.

"Now the eyes. It's all about the eyes. You can tell a lot about a person from just looking into their eyes. They need to look dark --- sunken."

I remembered the eyes of the old lady in the wheelchair who had reached out to me and I knew exactly what she was talking about.

"I can change the appearance of the eyes, but what someone will see when they look deep inside, is up to you. A person who is dying and has lost the will to live will lose that special sparkle."

It occurred to me that maybe I was selling this

gal short.

"The hair --- hmmm --- it's already gray and kind of mousey --- I think it will be OK."

"*Mousey?*"

After three hours in the makeup chair, she handed me a mirror.

"There! Let's see what you think."

"*HOLY CRAP!*"

I looked like the older brother of Gregory Grave, the host of Channel Nine's 1958 sci-fi show, *Shock Theatre*.

At that moment, the captain entered.

"Perfect," he said. "I don't think the doctor will be wasting any tests on you."

"So what's next?" I asked.

"You get to go home and study the dossier on Ray Braxton. In two days, you need to be him."

"Two days?"

"Yes, and don't shave. We don't want you messing up Sam's handiwork, and a couple of days of stubble would be consistent with a person who's given up.

"Plus, you have an appointment at Dr. Graves' office at nine o'clock, the day after tomorrow."

I should have slipped out the back entrance to the squad room, but old habits die hard.

I was about to leave through the front, when Officer Dooley entered.

He took one look and his eyes lit up like a Christmas tree.

"Oh my God!" he said. "Are they doing a remake of *Night Of The Living Dead*?"

That, of course, drew a crowd.

As I hurried out the door, someone shouted, "If you're going out with Lily Munster, tell her I said 'Hi'."

I always get this warm, fuzzy feeling when I can brighten someone's day.

On the way home, I noted that I was eliciting stares from the drivers of passing cars.

At one stoplight, I glanced at the lady in the car beside me and the look she had on her face was much like the one I get when I step in a pile of dog poo.

I arrived at my apartment building just as Dad was leaving.

"My God, Walt! You look like crap!"

"Thanks for noticing."

"Are you sick?"

I explained that it was just makeup and that I was on an undercover assignment and asked him to please keep it quiet.

He promised that he would, but as he walked

away, I heard him mutter, "My son, the stiff!"

Maggie was a different story. I didn't want to scare her to death, so I knocked on the door.

"Who is it?"

"Maggie, it's Walt."

"Did you lose your key?"

"No, I wanted to talk to you before I came in. I didn't want to shock you."

She threw open the door.

"What in the world ---"

She just stared for a moment and then she doubled over laughing.

"Walt Williams," she said between fits of giggles, "life with you is never dull.

"Get in here and tell me what you're up to now."

I shared our undercover operation with her over dinner.

When it was time for bed, she said, "I hope you don't have any amorous ideas. I'm just not sure I could handle it."

"I understand," I said.

We clicked off the light and the last thing I remembered before falling asleep was the thought that I should get extra compensation for loss of consortium.

I arrived at Dr. Graves's office at a quarter to nine.

The receptionist gave me some papers to fill out and told me to take a seat.

I noticed that when I sat, the people closest to me discreetly moved to seats across the room.

I didn't blame them. I certainly wouldn't have wanted to catch whatever it was that I had.

I turned in the papers along with the medical history files of the late Ray Braxton.

I returned to my seat and waited --- and waited --- and waited.

I have never understood why it's always that way in doctor's offices.

If I have an appointment for nine o'clock, why do I have to wait until ten?

If they can't see me until ten, why don't they just schedule my appointment for ten?

I just chalk it up to one of the great mysteries of life.

Finally, a nurse stepped into the room and called my name --- well, Ray Braxton's name.

She led me to an exam room, took my temperature and blood pressure, handed me one of those goofy gowns that open down the back and told me to strip.

I had forgotten about this part. If I had remembered, I might not have given in to the captain so easily.

I hate these stupid gowns.

No matter what you try to do, your ass hangs out the back.

To make matters worse, it's always as cold as a meat locker in the doctor's office and inevitably, after you're decked out in the thing, you have to wait another half hour before the doctor gets there.

The chairs are either metal or vinyl and it's like sitting on an ice cube.

I wondered how many other bare butts had sat on that chair and if they disinfected it between patients.

Probably not.

When the doctor finally entered, I was mildly surprised.

Since this guy was suspected of being part of a nefarious euthanasia scheme, I suppose I had pictured him as the mad scientist type.

Quite the contrary.

He was middle aged, medium build and had a

pleasant smile.

When I shook his extended hand, I found that it was warm.

That was a good sign. I definitely like doctors with warm hands.

"Mr. Braxton. I'm Dr. Graves.

"I've taken a moment to read your files and I suppose my first question is why you've come to see me. It would appear that you have been under a doctor's care."

"I have," I said, "but he told me that he had done all he could do for me. I guess I'm looking for another opinion."

"I totally understand," he said, "but after reviewing your medical history, I would have to concur with his findings. I'm afraid there's nothing more that I could suggest either."

"I was afraid of that and that's why I came to you. I have --- had --- a friend who was a patient of yours. He gave me your name and said that you have some --- ummm --- unconventional treatments for people in my condition."

"Oh really! And who was your friend?"

"Roger Beckham."

When I said the name, he stopped writing, paused and looked me squarely in the eyes.

I knew this moment was coming and I did my

best to duplicate the look that I saw in the eyes of the old lady in the wheelchair.

Finally, he spoke. "The treatment we prescribed for Mr. Beckham was, shall we say, somewhat rigorous. Are you sure that you're up for a treatment like that?"

We both knew that we both knew.

"I want it more than anything else," I said with conviction. "It's my last hope."

"Actually," Dr. Graves said, "I don't perform the procedure myself. We refer it to a specialist. I'll forward your file to him and if he can work you in, he will give you a call."

"Thank you," I said. "You have no idea how much this means to me."

"Actually, I do," he said as closed the door.

I sat there alone in the cold room and wondered what it had been like for Roger Beckham and Arthur Manning.

I, like them, had just scheduled my own death.

CHAPTER 8

Police business is a lot like the military --- hurry up and wait.

The bait was in the water and now it was time to sit back and wait for the fish to swim by.

It was possible that someone in the Final Exit Network was watching me, so I couldn't go home. I had to live in the department's 'safe house'.

Due to the delicate nature of my makeup, I had to shower with a bag over my head and even then, the perky Samantha had to drop by each day to give me a touch-up.

She always arrived in a hospice van to keep my cover intact.

After four days of not shaving, my mousey gray stubble made my appearance even more grizzly and grotesque.

Anytime I was out where there were people, my gaunt visage could part the crowd like Moses parting the Red Sea.

Little children would squeal and cling to their mommy's legs and I noticed that after leaving a checkout stand, the clerk would wipe everything down with antiseptic.

I supposed the captain was right; I was the closest thing they had to dead.

Maggie and I would talk on the phone.

She wanted to try to see me in some clandestine place, but I begged off, saying that it was against police procedure.

Actually, I was just afraid that if she saw me, that mental image would haunt her and jeopardize the plans Mr. Winkie had made for a happy homecoming.

I was bored out of my mind, so I took this opportunity to catch up on some reading and to watch some movies.

Since I was knee-deep in this euthanasia plot, I thought it might be a good idea to learn more about the most famous champion of the cause, Jack Kevorkian.

I found an HBO made-for-TV movie, titled, *You Don't Know Jack*, with Al Pacino as Kevorkian and Susan Sarandon as the leader of the Hemlock

93

Society.

It was a gut-wrenching, tear-jerking story from start to finish, filled with footage of terminally ill patients, suffering excruciating pain and begging Dr. Kevorkian to give them peace.

When it was all said and done, the message was, that to some, Kevorkian was an angel of mercy and to others he was a cold-blooded killer.

When it was over, Samantha had to re-do the makeup around my eyes.

On the evening of the fourth day, I received the call.

"Mr. Braxton?"

"Yes. This is Ray Braxton. Who is this?"

"You may simply call me Thanatos. Your physician referred you to me. I understand that you may be interested in a procedure."

"Yes, Sir. More than interested. I am ready. What do I have to do?"

"The first step is a consultation. I must be sure that you fully understand the finality of the procedure and explain the process.

"After we conclude the consultation, if you still wish to proceed and if I believe you are an acceptable candidate, I will give you further instructions."

"Fine. Where do you want me to go?"

"Nowhere, Mr. Braxton. I will come to you."

"My address is ---."

"Mr. Braxton, I'm quite aware of where you live.

"Shall we say eight o'clock tomorrow evening?"

"I'll be here --- and --- thank you."

As soon as our conversation ended, I called the captain to see if the equipment that the techs had installed had worked properly.

"We got it all," he said, "every word on tape. But they're good. We traced the number back to a disposable cell. We'll try to triangulate on it, but we'll probably find it in an alley dumpster somewhere."

"So what now?" I asked.

"Turn on the switch on the video feed we installed in the wall thermostat so that we can make sure it's still operational --- and for heaven's sake don't forget to turn it on tomorrow evening before he arrives.

"Other than that, just sit tight until tomorrow."

After I performed my tekkie chores, I flipped open the laptop and 'Googled' Thanatos.

Wikipedia told me that Thanatos was the god of death in ancient Greek mythology.

Our new Dr. Death, it would seem, had a flare for the dramatic.

I was a nervous wreck. I paced the floor, worrying that I might screw things up.

Of all the undercover work that I had done, this was, by far, the most difficult.

It's one thing to portray a goofy transvestite wearing a dress and a Tina Turner wig.

It's quite another to exude the emotions of a terminally ill patient intent on ending their life.

Watching the Kevorkian movie had helped give me some insight into the motivations of those poor suffering people.

I flipped on the switch to the video feed at seven thirty and tried to relax, but by eight o'clock my armpits were drenched with sweat.

At five past eight, there was a knock on the door.

One of the foibles of human nature is to conjure up images of people before actually meeting them.

In my minds eye, I had pictured Thanatos as a Mr. Spock, Star Trek kind of guy, pointy ears and all, but the man that stood before me was quite different.

My first impression was that Harrison Ford had just walked in the door --- the older, wrinkled Harrison Ford.

"Great," I thought. *"I'm going to be done in by Indiana Jones."*

"I am Thanatos," he said, extending his hand.

"Ray Braxton. Please come in."

When we were seated, he said, "Please tell me about yourself."

"There's not much left to tell. I'm alone and I'm dying of cancer. I'm guessing Dr. Graves shared my file with you."

"He did."

"Then that's about it. I have very little money, so what I have left to look forward to is to be institutionalized in a state hospital where they will pump me full of drugs and leave me to die a slow agonizing death.

"What little money I have left, I'd rather give to you for your services. I hope it will be enough."

Thanatos smiled. "We're not after your money. Our services are free to those who qualify."

"So do I qualify?" I asked expectantly.

He was about to answer when he saw the plastic cover of the *You Don't Know Jack* movie by the TV.

"I see you've been doing some homework," he said pointing to the CD.

"I thought it would help if I understood more about the process. After I watched it, I knew that this is what I want."

"You've made my job a lot easier," he said. "A part of what I do on my first visit is to make sure that the patient fully understands the finality of his decision."

"The movie helped me a lot. Dr. Kevorkian helped a lot of people. Did you know him?"

A far-away look filled Thanatos' eyes. "I did. My sister was patient #64 for Dr. Kevorkian.

"I treated her until, like you, there was no

98

more I could do. The pain was so intense that she begged to die. Jack took away her pain."

I was amazed that he had known the legend personally. I wanted to know more, so I pressed on.

"I just don't understand why there is so much opposition to what you are doing?"

"Dr. Jack was a pioneer ahead of his time," he said. "Deep seated beliefs do not change overnight.

"Did you know that ether was known in the fifteen hundreds but not used in surgery for over three hundred years. Surgeons operated on fully conscious people because the popular belief was that God wanted us to suffer for our sins."

"Unbelievable," I said.

"More recently, there was moral opposition to heart transplants on the premise that surgeons were playing 'God'."

"Maybe some day your practice will be as accepted as open heart surgery."

"We can always hope that society is moving toward enlightenment --- but --- back to your situation --- I think you are a good candidate. I will help you."

"Thank you. What do you want me to do?"

"You should get your affairs in order.

"I have documents for you to sign where you request the procedure we're offering, swear that it is being done of your own free will and holding all parties blameless.

"We also require that your final wish is that your body is to be cremated.

"Can you agree to all that?"

"Where do I sign? I'm ready."

"Also, if you have the means, you might want to put together some photos and music to enjoy at the end.

"We want this experience to be as pleasant and peaceful as possible. Some of our other patients have found it comforting."

"So when can we do this?" I asked. "It won't take long to get my affairs in order."

"Two nights from now --- same time --- eight o'clock."

"I'll be ready."

I signed the papers and he left.

I sat there in a daze.

I had just arranged for my death and it was a lot less hassle that when I tried to sign up for cable TV.

The phone rang. It was the captain.

"That was quite a performance, Walt. You had all of us believing that you were ready to croak. We got it all on tape."

"Captain, you saw the man. Did he look like a

murderer to you?"

"Walt, what I think and what you think doesn't matter. In the eyes of the law, the man is guilty of second-degree murder. It's our duty to enforce the law. Do you have a problem with that?"

"Uhhh --- no --- we're good."

When I hung up the phone I was anything but good.

After watching the Kevorkian movie and meeting Thanatos, I was beginning to wonder whether justice was really being served.

Lady Justice is depicted with a blindfold, but sometimes I wished that she could just slip it off for a moment so that she could see what was really going on.

In the next two days I tried to stay busy.

At Thanatos' suggestion, I put together a CD of photos that Maggie and I had taken on our honeymoon in Hawaii.

Obviously, I couldn't use ones that had Maggie, Willie or Mary, but we had taken dozens of photos of sunsets, beaches, rainbows and flowers.

The music I chose was *In This Life I Was Loved By You*, by Israel Kamakawiwo'ole.

As I put all this together, I tried to picture what this would feel like to a person who was actually planning his last moments.

I remembered a conversation I had heard between two old guys on the front porch of the Three Trails.

One of them said, "I wish I knew where I was gonna die."

The other guy asked, "Why in the world would you want to know that?"

"Because iffin I knew where it was, I wouldn't go there."

It had seemed stupid and inane at the time, but it made me wonder if knowing and planning might be better than a total surprise.

I couldn't decide.

At precisely eight o'clock there was a knock on the door.

I had seen cartoons that depicted the specter of the Grim Reaper standing at someone's door when their time had come.

I threw open my door but the messenger of death was not a shrouded ghoul with a scythe, but the smiling face of Indiana Jones.

I looked around the neighborhood before closing the door.

Somewhere out there, the captain and several officers were watching the video feed from a van.

Once Thanatos had set up the mercy machine, they would burst in and haul away the demon in handcuffs.

"Are you ready?" he asked.

"I am. I prepared a video like you suggested. Would you like to see it?"

"Certainly."

I opened the laptop, pressed the key and the images of a Hawaiian paradise flowed across the screen.

Iz's beautiful voice filled the room.

When it had played through, Thanatos said, "Hawaii is one of my favorite spots on earth.

"And that song --- it sounds as if there might have been someone special in your life."

"There was. And with your help, I'll be seeing her again soon."

"Then let's get to it."

He had me sit comfortably with the laptop where I could reach it.

When he was satisfied, he stood in front of me and looked me squarely in the eyes.

"We are almost ready. Before I bring in the Thanatron, I will ask you again. Is it your wish to die?"

"It is."

He stood staring for another full minute.

"Then I will get the machine. Make yourself comfortable."

I watched him leave and settled back into the chair.

I had expected him to be back in maybe five minutes, but after ten had passed, I began to worry.

When twenty minutes had passed, the door opened, but it was not Thanatos. It was the captain.

"Where's Thanatos?" I asked. "Have you arrested him?"

"Sorry, Walt. He's in the wind."

The flood of emotion that I felt at that moment overwhelmed me.

At first I thought it was disappointment.

Then I realized that it was relief.

CHAPTER 9

Everyone associated with the Dr. Death operation was bummed out.

We went back to the precinct and played the videos of my meetings with Thanatos over and over again, trying to pinpoint what had spooked the guy.

Even the department psychologist thought that I had played a convincing part.

We came to a dead end and I announced that I was going to head home to my sweet wife.

I hadn't seen her in a week.

Dooley, ever vigilant for an opportunity to poke fun at the old man said, "Are you really going home like that? Unless Maggie is into necrophilia, you probably won't be getting any."

I looked in the mirror.

For once, he was right on.

I had been a walking corpse for so long that I had nearly forgotten how ghastly I had become.

I went into the locker room, stripped and headed for the shower.

I stood there for the longest time letting the hot water pour over my body --- my first shower in a week without a bag over my head.

I watched as Samantha's handiwork swirled down the drain.

I shaved off the stubble and when I looked in the mirror, I was almost human again.

I called Maggie and told her that I was on the way home.

She told me to hurry.

She met me at the door and it was one of those special occasions where very few words were exchanged.

We tumbled into bed and held each other close.

My work had made me come face-to-face with the specter of death, but at that moment, I was so glad to be alive.

When we were both spent, the words to Iz's beautiful ballad filled my mind.

"If it all falls apart, I will know deep in my heart

"The only dream that mattered had come true.

"In this life, I was loved by you."

The next morning, I was enjoying a leisurely breakfast.

The captain had told me to take the day off to decompress.

I had just wolfed down a plate of Maggie's pancakes and was ready for my second cup of coffee when I opened the newspaper.

There, in blazing headlines, I read;

"Dr. Death Defies Police Undercover Operation!"

The article stated that the police had confirmed that a euthanasia ring was operating in the Kansas City area and that at least two of their victims had been found.

It went on to say that an undercover officer had made contact with 'Dr. Death', and had scheduled a procedure, but the plan fell apart before the killer could be apprehended.

I was stunned. The operation, as was typical of all undercover work, was classified.

107

No one was supposed to be privy to the information except the officers involved, but the article gave specific details of the bust gone wrong.

I showed the headline to Maggie.

"I have to get to the precinct."

"So much for a day of rest," she said as I hurried out the door.

I went straight to the captain's office.

"I suppose you saw the paper," he said as I entered.

"I thought this was hush-hush," I said, tossing the paper on his desk.

"It was," he replied. "This didn't come through official channels --- someone leaked it!"

"But, who? --- Why?"

"I wish I knew. Now our chances of cracking that euthanasia ring are slim and none. Since its been broadcast that we're onto them, they'll probably bring their activities to a halt.

"And that's not my only problem," he said clicking on the TV with his remote.

"Watch this."

The screen filled with a shot of the J.C. Nichols fountain on the Country Club Plaza.

Two very vocal groups were congregated on opposite sides of the fountain.

One group carried placards with the

108

inscription, 'Death With Dignity', and the other group carried signs saying, 'Care-Not Killing!'

The two groups were shouting at one another and were being kept apart only by a line of my fellow officers.

The cameraman focused on a reporter who was interviewing one of the protestors.

"Are you part of an organized group?" the reporter asked.

"Some of us belong to the Nightingale Alliance, but others are just concerned citizens appalled at the atrocities being committed in our city."

"The folks on the other side of the fountain," the reporter said, pointing across the way, "say that the individual has the right to control his own destiny and make life and death choices. What are your arguments against euthanasia?"

"Where do I start?

"From the moral and religious perspective, euthanasia fundamentally undermines the basis of law and public morality. It weakens society's respect for the sanctity of life.

"To kill oneself or to get someone else to do it for us is to deny God and deny God's rights over our lives."

"Your opponents might say that this religious

point of view is a conflict of church and state and that the individual has the right to choose. Are there grounds other than from a religious perspective, to oppose euthanasia?"

"Once the practice becomes accepted," she replied, "it will be difficult to control.

"Abortion is a case in point. Thirty years ago, abortion was permitted only to save the life and health of the mother. But now, the 'right-to-choose' advocates have twisted it into abortion on demand.

"I know it might be unthinkable in today's world, but Adolph Hitler murdered seventy thousand disabled people, labeling them 'useless eaters'.

"It's not difficult to see how 'right-to-die' could be transformed into 'duty-to-die'."

"Why are you here today?"

"There is a serial killer in our city, murdering people under the guise of humanitarianism. The morning paper told how this cold-blooded killer slipped through the fingers of the police.

"We're here to let this murderer know that we are enraged by his actions and to demand that the police use whatever resources are necessary to bring this criminal to justice."

The captain switched off the TV.

"See what I mean?"

"What are you going to do?"

110

"First, try to find the leak. I'm going to talk to the reporter at the *Star*, but I'm betting he won't reveal his source.

"Then, try to contain the fallout from our aborted sting and come up with another plan to bring Dr. Death to justice, while keeping these two groups from tearing one another apart."

"Well, good luck with all of that," I said with disgust. "I'm outta here!"

When I returned home, my old friend, Willie was just getting home, himself.

He had a package under his arm.

"Hey, Willie. Been shopping?"

"Well, not 'zactly. I been to see Miss Larue."

"Another one of your paramours?"

"My para what?"

"Never mind. What's in the package?"

"Got me a wee-gee board."

"Oh, you mean a Ouija board!"

"Dat's what I said, a wee-gee board. Got it from Miss Larue."

"And what, exactly, are you planning to do

with it?"

"Talk to my dead folks. Miss Larue showed me how.

"Since I learned about 'em, I been wantin' to know more, so I figgered de bes' way was to talk to 'em direct."

Willie was raised by an old maid aunt and had been on the streets by himself since he was a teenager.

He knew a little about his mom, but he never met his dad who was killed in WWII.

He knew nothing at all about his grandparents or any of his distant relatives until a few months ago.

His last living relative had died and Willie was the beneficiary of her estate, such as it was.

Included was an old family Bible that held a history of Willie's ancestors.

They turned out to be quite a colorful bunch, in more ways than one.

Willie had been fascinated by their story and often talked about them to anyone who would listen.

"So where did you come up with this Miss Larue?" I asked.

"Louie de Lip tole me 'bout her. She got a place down on Prospect where she reads palms an' shit like dat."

"Oh, well, if Louie the Lip recommended her,

she must be legit."

"Dat's wot I was thinkin."

"Willie, I'm kidding! You know Louie is a con artist. He's probably in cahoots with Miss What's Her Name. How much did she charge you for that thing?"

"Fifty bucks."

"You can get them at Buy Mart for twenty."

"Damn! I gotta have me a talk wif Louie!

"So you don' think this wee-gee stuff works?"

"I'm quite sure it doesn't. It's a parlor game."

"Well, I know'd you was involved wif all dis death stuff and it kinda got me thinking about my kin ----."

"How did you know what I was doing?"

"Yo pappy tole me. Den I axed Maggie an she tole me de same ting."

"So I'm guessing that everybody in the building knows what I've been doing?"

"Well sho. You don't tink you can be gone a whole week and nobody miss you."

So much for undercover.

"Tell you what, Willie. I've got a day off. If you really want to know more about your family, I'll take you to the genealogy center and we can do some research."

"Oh, dat's jus' great! You makin' fun of my

wee-gee an' now you want me to go an' talk to your genie."

"That's not --- oh, never mind --- let's just go --- I'll explain it on the way."

On the way back to the apartment, my cell phone came to life.

Ox had showed me how to add custom ring tones and I had chosen the theme from *Dragnet*.

I thought that was appropriate for an old cop with a fifties mentality.

Willie was startled when the phone boomed,

"Dunn - de - dunn - dunn. Dunn - de - dunn - dunn. Dunnnnnnnn!"

"Wot de hell is dat?"

I picked up the phone. "Walt Williams here."

"Walt. This is Officer Murphy. Isn't the Three Trails one of yours?"

"Yes. I'm afraid it is. Why?"

"We had a report of a shot fired --- thought you might want to know."

"I'm on the way."

When we arrived, Murphy's black and white was parked at the curb.

Mary and a half-dozen residents were milling around in the yard.

"What's up?" I asked.

"One of the tenants heard what sounded like a shot coming from old man Friedman's room," Mary said. "So he called 911."

"When I arrived," Murphy said, "the door was locked. I knew you were on the way so I figured I'd wait rather than bust the door."

"I appreciate that," I said. "Willie, do you have your picks?"

"Don't go nowhere without 'em."

Murphy, Willie and I trudged upstairs to Mort Friedman's room.

I knocked but there was no answer, so I gave Willie the nod.

He did his magic and when we pushed the door open, my worst fears were realized.

Friedman lay sprawled on the old mattress in a pool of red that had soaked through and was dripping into a grisly puddle on the floor.

Brain matter, bits of scull and blood were spattered on the wall behind the bed.

A snub-nosed .38 lay beside his limp hand.

This wasn't my first suicide. In three years, I

115

had seen deaths by carbon monoxide, poison, and hanging, but gunshots are always the worst.

This was the first I had seen that involved someone I knew.

I heard the door open across the hall and old man Feeney peered out.

"Old Mort offed hisself, didn't he? I knowed he was gonna do it."

"How did you know that?" Murphy asked. "Did he actually tell you?"

"Nope. But I knew he had been feelin' poorly and that he took hisself to the free clinic.

"They told him that he was all eat up inside and there warn't nothing they could do.

"He didn't have no kin around here and I guess he figured there warn't much left to look forward to.

"I knew he got his Social Security check the other day. Musta used it to buy the gun.

"I liked old Mort. We used to play checkers."

"I'll send for the meat wagon," Murphy said.

I looked at Friedman's tortured body missing the top of its scull.

Just another old man ending his existence in the tiny room of a sleazy boarding house.

I'd be willing to bet that it wouldn't get even a line of print in the *Star*.

Then I thought of the bodies of Beckham and Manning that had been found in peaceful repose, and the papers were screaming for the capture of the terrible villain who had assisted these men in their final act.

I wondered if those who were condemning Dr. Death were to see the body of Mort Friedman, would they still feel the same way?

All three were just as dead, but the means to that end were a world apart.

Willie hadn't stirred since we made our grisly discovery.

Finally, he spoke.

"Mr. Walt. Do I has to clean dis up? I'se willin' to do mos' anything, but I don't know if'n I can do dis."

"No, Willie. I wouldn't ask you to do that. There are companies that specialize in this sort of thing."

"Thanks, Mr. Walt. Mort was my frien' too."

The next morning, Ox and I were on our regular patrol.

"I missed you, buddy," he said. "Sorry to hear about your tenant."

"With you gone, I had to ride with a young greenhorn all week."

I guess he'd forgotten that just three years ago, I was an old greenhorn.

"Yea, it's good to be back. I missed you too. Playing a dead guy wasn't my idea of fun and games."

"Too bad that the guy skipped," he said. "Any idea why?"

"No, we've been over the tapes and everything was going according to plan ---."

Just then the radio crackled.

"Car 54. Are you close to the Waldo neighborhood?"

I picked up the mike. "About five minutes away."

"Proceed to the seventy-three hundred block of Madison. Another DOA. Looks like your Dr. Death has struck again."

When we arrived, the EMT's and the coroner were already on the scene.

The same EMT that we had seen at the Beckham and Manning homes met us at the door.

118

"Another old guy," he said. "A neighbor who checks in on him every morning found him just sitting in his recliner --- just like the other guys.

"Too bad that creep got away the other night. If you had caught him, this old man might still be alive."

"Well thanks, Mr. Sensitive," I thought. *"That's just what I needed to brighten my day."*

The coroner was completing his examination when we entered the room.

I looked at the body. At first glance, it did indeed appear to be just like the two previous deaths.

"Hi Doc," I said. "Can you determine cause of death?"

"Not until I can get him on the table. I did find a syringe mark in his arm that would be consistent with what we found on Arthur Manning."

I noticed a black liquid on the wood floor under the victim's feet.

"What's that black stuff," I asked.

"Most likely, urine. Sometimes the bowels or bladder release upon death."

"But why is it black? In my experience, urine is yellow --- you know the old saying --- don't eat the yellow snow."

"Again, Mr. Funny Man, I won't know until I have it analyzed, but I'll be sure to note your comment for the lab boys."

Something else about the body didn't seem quite right.

It was the face.

I had seen the faces of Beckham and Manning and I remembered thinking how peaceful they looked.

This guy looked anything but peaceful --- in fact --- his expression was that of a man who had died of fright.

"If you're through with your examination, do you mind if I take a look at the body?"

"Help yourself, officer."

I snapped a photo with my new camera phone and then I had Ox help me move the body forward far enough to pull his wallet from his back pocket.

"Driver's license says he's Jack Fredricks. Seventy-five years old --- here's his AARP card --- ahhh, and here's a card with a doctor Millikan's number."

"Yea," Ox said, "but do you see what's missing?"

I looked again. "No cash and no credit cards!"

"That doesn't necessarily mean anything," Ox said, "but it's worth looking into."

"How about you taking a look around the house while I call the doctor," I said.

Dr. Millikan was not one of the doctor's we had profiled in our investigation, but it was possible that we could have missed one.

When Milliken came on the line, I identified myself.

"Is Jack Fredricks one of your patients?"

"Yes, I've known Jack for years."

"By any chance was he dying?"

"We're all dying, officer, but if you're asking if he had a terminal disease, the answer is 'no'. He had angina but we were keeping it under control with medication."

By the time I hung up, I was convinced that Jack Fredricks would not have been an acceptable candidate for Thanatos.

Ox returned from making the rounds of the house.

"Couldn't find a thing," he said.

"What do you mean?"

"I mean I couldn't find anything of value --- no watches, no jewelry --- it's like the guy had absolutely nothing. But there was also no sign of forced entry and nothing was disturbed or damaged."

We returned to the living room just as the EMT's were loading the body onto the gurney.

I noticed a slip of paper protruding from a pants pocket.

"Hang on a minute," I said, retrieving the paper.

It was a cash register receipt for a caramel frappuccino from Starbucks at the Ward Parkway shopping center.

The time stamp on the receipt was the night before at seven twenty.

"Doc," I said, "have you established a time of death?"

"My best guess at this point would be between nine and midnight last night."

I pulled Ox aside.

"This isn't the work of Dr. Death. We've got a copycat!"

CHAPTER 10

After the EMT's were gone and the body was on the way to the morgue, I called the captain and told him that we needed to talk.

He told us to come on in.

"So what did you find?" he asked.

"It's not Thanatos," I said. "It's a copycat.

"Somebody either got an idea from the newspaper or, even worse, had inside information about the other euthanasias, killed this old guy and made it look like the work of Dr. Death --- only it wasn't! It was a robbery, pure and simple."

"Just what are you basing all this on?" he asked.

"Well, first, his wallet was empty of any money or credit cards and Ox found no valuables around the house."

"There could be a reasonable explanation for that," the captain said. "I'm sure you're familiar with the old saying, "You can't take it with you." Maybe knowing he was going to die, he just gave everything away --- maybe to charity."

"Yes, but there's more. I talked to his doctor and he wasn't terminally ill. I know what I had to go through just to get Thanatos to consider me. He just didn't fit their criteria.

"I'd be willing to bet that the autopsy will show that potassium chloride was not the cause of death."

"You could be right," the captain said. "Finish your patrol and I'll let you know when the coroner's report is in."

We finished our shift without further incident and were just clocking out when the captain appeared.

"Walt, Ox, I need a minute."

When we were in his office he turned and grinned.

124

"Looks like I may have to transfer you to the CSI unit as a forensics expert. You were right."

"So the coroner's report is in?"

"Yes, and the cause of death, as you predicted, was not potassium chloride. Fredricks died of asphyxia. He was smothered."

"No wonder he looked scared to death," I said. "What a horrible way to die."

"Then what about the needle mark in his arm," Ox asked.

"And the black liquid on the floor," I added.

"Fredricks had been injected with something called methocarbamol. It's a muscle relaxant. He had been given a large enough dose to render him nearly unconscious and certainly unable to offer any resistance.

"The black liquid was indeed urine. That's one of the side effects of methocarbamol. It temporarily turns urine a black or brown color."

"So are you on board with the copycat idea?" I asked.

"Right now, that's the theory."

After we left the captain's office, I pulled Ox aside.

"Do you have any plans for the evening?"

"I'm a single guy with no current girlfriend. What do you think?"

"Let's take a trip out to the Ward Parkway Center Shopping Mall. Do you remember that slip of paper I pulled from Fredrick's pocket?"

"Yea, didn't you turn that in?"

"Not yet. I want to check out a theory."

"Let's do it."

I called Maggie on the way out and told her that I would be running late.

She sounded a bit peeved, but said that she would save a plate for me in the oven.

The Ward Parkway Mall runs from State Line Road on the west to Ward Parkway on the east. It's a two-story structure, but most of the shops are on the second level, which is accessed from the State Line side.

There is also an entrance on the lower level of the Ward Parkway side. A long corridor leads to an escalator that transports shoppers to the upper level.

We entered from the Ward Parkway side. The long corridor was virtually empty.

The escalator took us to the second floor. I checked a directory and saw that Starbucks was at the far end of the Mall.

The Mall was busy, but not overcrowded. I noticed that there were a lot of seniors, walking and peering into the shops.

Starbucks was busy, as usual, and patrons were lined up three deep to pay five bucks for a cup of coffee.

We waited in line and when it was our turn, a pleasant young man greeted us.

I showed him my badge and told him we'd like to ask him a few questions.

"Sure," he said. "How can I help?"

"Were you working last night?"

"Yep. I go to school during the day and work the night shift here."

I pulled out my cell phone to show him Fredrick's photo that I had taken at the crime scene.

"Have you seen this man in here?"

He looked at the phone.

"Well first, that's no dude. And second, she's pretty hot for an old gal."

I looked at the phone and there, in all her glory, was Maggie --- buck-naked.

"Oh crap!" I thought. *"Maggie's going to kill me!"*

I had promised her that I would erase the photo, but nobody had showed me how.

I looked at Ox who was doing his best to hold it together.

"Ain't technology great!" he said.

I regained my composure, scrolled through the photo album and held up the correct picture.

"How about this one?"

"Sure. That's Jack Fredricks. He's a regular --- Monday, Wednesday and Friday --- caramel frappuccino --- no whipped cream.

"He don't look so good."

"That's because he's dead."

"Old Jack is dead. DAMN!"

"Were the two of you close?"

"Not really. But he was a hell of a tipper. He'd hand over a ten spot each time. Then he'd wink and say "Keep the change". He always had a big wad of cash in his wallet."

I looked at Ox and he nodded.

Jack Fredricks had flashed his cash one too many times.

"So he was in here last night?" Ox asked.

"Yea, about seven, I think."

"Was he with anyone?"

"Not that I could see. He just got his drink and left."

We thanked the clerk and as we headed back to the car, I commented, "I'll bet this won't be the last of these copycat murders."

I just didn't know that it would be so soon.

It had been a long day and I was looking forward to getting home to Maggie to enjoy what was left of the evening.

I had just finished with the plate that Maggie had kept warm for me in the oven, when I heard a knock on the door.

"*Oh great! What now?*" I thought.

I opened the door and looked into the faces of my five tenants.

Just what I needed.

"And to what do I owe the honor of this visit?" I asked.

"Do you still have those DNR things we gave you?" Dad asked. "You know, where we gave you permission to pull our plugs?"

"Sure," I said. "They're in my file cabinet."

"Could you get them? We want to add some stuff."

"Really? What kind of stuff?"

Just then, Maggie came up behind me.

"For heaven's sake, Walt. Don't make them stand out in the hall. Invite them in."

"But it's getting late," I protested.

"Yea, I know it's late," Dad said, "but this is important, Sonny."

After we were all seated in the living room, I said, "OK, what's so urgent?"

"Well," Dad replied, "none of us are spring chickens. And with all this death stuff that's been going on and with old Mort over at the hotel --- well, we thought we should do some planning. You know, just in case one of us is next."

"What kind of planning?"

"Walt, you're my next of kin. What are you going to do with me when I croak?"

"I don't know. I guess I hadn't really thought about it."

"SEE! We need to figure this stuff out."

"We've been doing some research," Jerry said, "about how different cultures deal with their old folks.

"We read about how the Eskimos set their old people adrift on icebergs and how some tribes light a big funeral pyre."

"Well first, we're a little short on icebergs here in midtown and second, Kansas City has a no-burning ordinance, so I think we can rule out those two possibilities."

"That wasn't the point," Dad said. "You obviously haven't given much thought as to how you're going to dispose of my remains."

"No, I'll have to admit that hasn't been at the top of my to-do list."

"We've done some checking," the Professor said, "and it would seem that our two most viable options are cremation and burial."

"I just don't know if I could stand being buried," Bernice said. "Just thinking about being put in a box and buried in the ground with all those worms and bugs and crawly things. It gives me the creeps."

"Now Bernice," Dad said, "we've been over this. They don't just dig a hole and toss you in. You're placed in a casket, and the casket is put in a vault. No worms --- no bugs."

"Well that's better, but all that dirt on top of me --- I just don't know."

"Another consideration," the Professor said, "is the cost. A modest casket, a vault and opening the grave would run about eight thousand. By comparison, cremation and a nice urn would run about fifteen hundred."

"Plus, you have to buy a burial plot and a headstone," Jerry said. "I know I don't have that kind of money."

"Cremation is the way I want to go," Dad said. "Then just go to a high hill and scatter my ashes to the four winds.

"I've been all over this great country, first in the service and then as a trucker. I can't see spending eternity stuck in a hole somewhere. Let the wind scatter me to the far corners of the earth."

I thought that would certainly be a fitting end for my Dad, and if we had a memorial service, the song that I would select to commemorate his life would be Ricky Nelson's *Travelin' Man*.

"Well I'm a travelin' man; made a lot of stops, all over this world.

And in every port I own the heart of at least one lovely girl."

Then Willie spoke up.

"I got me a question 'bout dis cremation stuff. What about ghosts? Say I might want to hang around a while and haunt some folks. Can I still do it if I ain't nothin' but ashes? The ghosts I've seen always come back in bodies."

"That's an easy one," Jerry said. "Buried ghosts come back in their bodies, but cremated ghosts come back in white sheets."

132

"I guess that makes sense," Willie said. "I've seen both kinds."

"But you don't EVER want to goose one of those ghosts," Jerry said solemnly.

"How come?"

"Cause you'll get 'sheet' on your finger!"

"You're just sick!" Bernice said.

"And while we're on the subject," Jerry said, "here's one for you.

"If a ram is a male sheep and an ass is a donkey, how come a ram in the ass is a goose?"

"Can't you EVER be serious?" Bernice said.

"OK. I've got another question," Jerry said. "If Willie and I were both cremated, would our ashes be different colors?"

"That is an interesting observation," the Professor said.

I could tell that the conversation had drifted to the absurd and it was getting later by the minute.

"Just stay here. I'll get your living wills. You can take them and make whatever notations you want about the disposition of your remains.

"Just don't bring them back tonight. I'm going to bed!"

The next day was uneventful, but on the second day after Fredrick's body was discovered, we heard another call come through the radio.

We were patrolling Midtown, but when I heard that a body had been discovered in the eighty-three hundred block of Belleview, I radioed that we were also proceeding to the scene.

The black and white that had taken the call was already there when we arrived.

The responding officer was surprised to see us.

"So what are you guys doing here. I don't remember signaling for the Dynamic Duo."

"Very funny," I said. "Ox and I have responded to three of these calls and we just wanted to compare this scene with the ones we worked."

"Knock yourself out," he said. "Martha Wallace --- seventy-eight --- lives alone. Found her in her rocker. No signs of a struggle or forced entry. Any ideas?"

I looked at the body.

"Tell the coroner to look for something called methocarbamol and I'll bet you lunch at Mel's that she was smothered."

"Whoa! You seem pretty sure about all that."

"Just check it out. Mind if we look around the house?"

134

"Help yourself."

We made the rounds and ended up in her bedroom. Her purse was on a nightstand.

Ox opened the purse and found her wallet. Sure enough --- no credit cards or cash.

I saw a white slip of paper and opened it up.

It was a cash receipt from the Target store at the Ward Parkway Mall.

The time stamp was seven forty-five the previous night.

Our copycat was stalking seniors and abducting them at the Mall.

We had to figure out how.

CHAPTER 11

The captain was staring at the two register receipts.

I could tell that he was pissed.

"So you're telling me that you lifted evidence from two crime scenes and didn't log it in?"

"It's all on me," I said. "Ox had no idea.

"I had a theory and I wanted to check it out and I think I'm right. Someone is abducting these old folks from the Mall, driving them to their homes, robbing them and making their murders look like it was the work of Dr. Death --- but they're not getting it right."

"You seem to have a way of circumventing normal procedure," he said. "I hope one day it doesn't come back and bite you in the butt."

"Yes, sir. I hear you."

"If you're right," the captain said, "we need to focus on that Mall. Whoever is doing this has killed twice in three days.

"Has there been any activity on the credit cards taken from the victim's purse and wallet?" I asked.

"Not on the credit cards, but the thieves used ATM machines to clean out their bank accounts."

"Was there anything you could use from the surveillance cameras at the ATM's?" Ox asked.

"Not a thing," he replied. "The guy was wearing a ball cap pulled low over his face. We never got a look.

"Back to the Mall thing. Do you guys have any ideas?"

"Actually, we do," Ox said. "Those indoor malls are filled with seniors. It's the perfect place for them to exercise --- it's warm in the winter and cool in the summer --- so they show up in droves. They walk and shop and talk to each other --- easy pickings for someone targeting seniors."

"So," I said, "we need to get our own seniors in there --- some really old guys who fit the profile.

"There are at least a half dozen ways in and out of the mall, so we would need officers in plain clothes to cover the exits. With eight to ten pairs of eyes in there, we've got a good chance to catch the guy if he tries it again."

"I like the idea, but you're the oldest guy we have and unless we let Samantha have another go at you, you really don't fit the profile."

"I think I can come up with some old dudes who'd love to help."

"You're not talking civilians, I hope?"

"Where else are you going to find eighty year-old guys?

"All they have to do is walk around the mall and flash a little cash. We'll have eyes on them all the time. Besides, these guys have worked with me before."

"Why do I let you talk me into these hair-brained schemes?"

"Because they work --- well --- most of the time."

"Heaven help us!"

A casual observer would never have guessed that the little group gathered in the Armour Boulevard apartment was one of Lady Justice's premier crime-fighting teams.

It consisted of two octogenarians, a scrawny, gray-headed black guy and a sixty-eight year old cop.

I had just showed them crime scene photos of Jack Fredricks and Martha Wallace.

"That's horrible!" Dad said. "Count me in! We gotta nail those bastards!"

"I, too, would love to participate," the Professor said. "It's not often that men of our age have the opportunity to serve in law enforcement."

"So wot do we gotta do?" Willie asked.

"Dad and the Professor will simply stroll around the mall --- exercising like dozens of others. Every so often they will flash a wad of bills --- supplied by the department --- to buy coffee or some little trinket."

"Wot 'bout me?" Willie asked.

"You'll be dressed as mall maintenance. You'll sweep floors, empty trash cans --- stuff like that."

"How come I got to be a janitor?" he asked indignantly. "Sounds like racial profilin' to me."

"Quite the contrary," I said. "That's one of the most important jobs. The janitor thing is just your cover. You're actually part of the surveillance team. It gives you the opportunity to keep your eyes on Dad and the Professor."

"Well, in dat case, I guess it's OK."

139

My team was on board and we were ready to roll.

By five o'clock the next day, we had everything set up.

There were officers in plainclothes milling around all the interior entrances and officers in unmarked cars watched the exterior exits.

Willie was busy pushing a big broom while Dad and the Professor casually strolled the promenade.

If the guy struck again, we would be ready.

Surveillance work can be mind numbing. After three hours of watching mothers drag screaming kids through the mall and old fat ladies waddling laps, I was about to scream.

Ox came up beside me. "It's quiet and I'm starved. Let's break for a bite to eat."

I was ready.

The only place close by was a fast food franchise called *Five Guys Burgers And Fries.*

I had seen their ads on TV, but had never eaten there.

The idea of a juicy burger and greasy French fries was actually appealing.

It didn't exactly fit with my current diet, but I figured that considering all the fiber and other organic stuff that Maggie had been feeding me lately, a little grease to lubricate the old poop chute couldn't hurt.

When we walked in, the first thing I saw was a sign that read, *"100% Fresh Beef ----No Fillers --- No Preservatives --- Our Menu Is Transfat Free"*

"Well, there you go," I thought. *"Maggie would be proud and I can eat guilt-free."*

I ordered my burger and fries and while I waited for my order, I noticed copies of news clippings on the wall.

One said, *"The Best $5 Burger A Man Can Eat"* GQ Magazine.

Another said, *"Rated #1 Burger for Lunch in NYC."*

I had ordered a single bacon cheeseburger with lettuce and tomato. Ox ordered a double with everything.

When Ox unwrapped his burger, the thing was so big, there was no way I could ever open my mouth wide enough to eat it, but somehow, Ox managed.

He took a bite, swallowed and said, "Damn!

That's good!"

I took my first bite, and he was right. It was damn good.

We had nearly finished wolfing down our burgers and cajun fries, when the manager approached.

"How was your lunch?" he asked. "Can I get you anything else?"

I was about to answer when I heard a siren and saw lights flashing in the parking lot.

An ambulance pulled up to the curb and two paramedics jumped out and unloaded a gurney.

I turned to Ox, "I wonder if we missed something?"

The manager, overhearing our conversation, said, "Oh, that's nothing to be concerned about. We see them at least once a week. It's the walkers --- the seniors --- every so often one falls or has a spell with their heart.

"Come to think of it though --- this is the third one this week."

I thanked the manager and we took off after the gurney.

We caught up with it at the far end of the mall.

An elderly lady riding up the escalator didn't make the dismount cleanly and had taken a tumble.

The paramedics were checking her out but she seemed to have recovered.

"Do you need to go to the emergency room?" one asked.

"Heavens, no," she replied. "I'm just a clumsy old woman. I'll be OK."

They packed up their gurney and left.

"False alarm," I said to Ox.

The mall shut down at ten.

We packed it in and called it a day.

The second day was a carbon copy of the first.

Lots of walkers, but no stalkers.

The captain stopped by the mall just before closing.

"No action, I guess?" he asked.

"Everything's quiet," I said.

"I'm sorry, Walt, but I'm going to have to pull the plug. This operation requires a lot of manpower and with the weekend coming up, I'm going to need the officers elsewhere. We gave it a shot, but I'm afraid it's time to move on."

143

I was disappointed, but I couldn't argue with his logic.

Since I had been tied up with the mall operation all week, Maggie and I hadn't had much time to spend together.

I had promised her a 'date' and I was determined to make good on it.

We slept late, ate a leisurely breakfast and after lunch, took in an afternoon movie.

We stopped for a bite to eat after the movie and then headed home for, what I hoped would be, a romantic end to our day together.

On the way up the stairs, we met Bernice in the hall.

She seemed surprised. "Oh, I thought that might be your dad."

I looked at my watch. It was almost nine o'clock.

"It's late. What is Dad doing out at this hour?"

"Well, he and Willie left about five o'clock. They said they had some unfinished business at the mall. I thought he'd be back by now."

I turned to Maggie, "Oh crap! They're hot-dogging it! They're out there by themselves with no backup. Call Ox and have him meet me at the mall. I gotta go."

I kissed her and headed to the Ward Parkway Mall.

By the time I arrived, things were starting to shut down.

Most of the walkers were long gone. A few last-minute shoppers were checking out their purchases.

I had come in on the second floor from the State Line side.

I looked down the near-empty promenade and about midway, I saw my dad being led away by a younger man.

He struggled and the man struck him in the head.

"DAD!" I yelled, and sprinted toward them.

I had just taken a few steps when a black streak in a maintenance uniform charged and struck the man with a broom handle.

145

The man released Dad and sprinted toward the far end of the mall.

Dad fell to the floor.

I yelled at Willie, "You take care of Dad. I'll get this guy."

The man had run to the far end of the mall. The promenade made a sharp turn to the right into another corridor that led to the movie theatre and the escalator that went down to the Ward Parkway entrance.

I rounded the corner expecting to see the guy barreling down the escalator, but there was no one in sight.

There was nothing there but a playground area with miniature cars, trains and other stuff that kids could ride for fifty cents a pop, a stairway up to the theatre entrance and the escalator.

The guy was nowhere in sight.

I walked past the playground and peered over the rail to the corridor below.

I saw movement out of the corner of my eye and turned in time to see the man charging toward me.

He had been hiding in the cab of a small rocket ship.

I raised my arm to ward off the blow, but it was too late.

I took the blow to the side of my head and saw the proverbial stars.

As I was falling, I saw another man coming up the escalator.

They each grabbed an arm and drug me down to the corridor below, where a gurney was waiting.

They hoisted me onto the gurney.

I tried to struggle, but I was still woozy from the blow to the head.

One guy said, "Hold him down so I can get this into him."

The second guy pinned my shoulders back and the next thing I saw was a syringe coming toward me.

It was in the hand of the EMT from the Dr. Death crime scenes.

He jabbed the needle into my arm and pushed the plunger.

Within seconds, my jaw went slack, my eyes rolled back in my head and no matter how hard I tried, I couldn't move my arms and legs.

They shoved the gurney into the waiting ambulance and the last thing I saw before they closed the door was Willie running down the corridor.

I felt the ambulance accelerate away.

I just hoped that Willie had arrived in time to see them load me in the van. It was my only chance.

I felt the ambulance come to a stop.

When the door opened, I recognized where they had taken me --- the morgue!

The place was deserted at that time of night, so no one saw them wheel me into the autopsy room.

I was still under the influence of the drug they had given me and I could barely keep my eyelids open.

Maybe I should have closed them. What I saw filled me with horror.

They were opening the door of a negative cold chamber.

I remembered touring the morgue as part of my academy training.

The technician had showed us the bodies of the deceased that were being kept in the cold chambers prior to autopsy.

The positive chamber's temperature was kept just under forty degrees for bodies that were to be cut open soon.

The negative chamber's temperature was a frosty ten degrees, which was low enough to freeze

148

the body and halt decomposition.

I saw the rolling slab slide out of the chamber next to my gurney.

One guy took my feet and the EMT grabbed me under the arms, and they lifted me onto the cold slab.

The EMT looked into my face. "This may not be the way Dr. Death would have done it, but you'll be just as dead."

As they were rolling the slab into the chamber, I heard the second guy say, "Goodnight, copper. Don't let the bedbugs bite! --- Oh, wait --- there's no bedbugs in there. They're all frozen!"

I heard them both laughing as the door slammed shut.

Their words were muffled, but I heard one of them say. "Time to ditch the ambulance and get out of town. We made enough on the last two jobs to hold us for awhile."

"I agree," the other said. "You follow me in your car while I ditch the ambulance, then we'll pick up our stuff from our room at the Randolph and split."

Then there was nothing but silence --- and total darkness --- and bitter cold.

I've never been a phobia kind of guy --- well, heights make me really dizzy, but it's never kept me

149

from going up on ferris wheels.

Maggie is kind of claustrophobic and tends to avoid tight places, but me, not so much.

Then, from somewhere within that big book in my brain that stores all the meaningless crap, I remembered that taphephobia was the fear of vivisepulture, --- of being buried alive.

I'd never paid much attention to it because, really, what were the chances of being buried alive?

Just my luck. I couldn't win five bucks on a scratcher ticket, but it seemed that I had just won the vivisepulture lottery.

The good news was that the drug that they had injected was beginning to wear off.

The bad news was that the numbing cold was seeping into every joint in my body.

At ten degrees Fahrenheit, I knew it wouldn't be long before I became a Walter Williams popsicle.

With a great deal of pain, I lifted my arms and began to feel the boundaries of my confinement.

There was maybe a foot of space on either side and over my head --- just enough room to maneuver my arms.

Everything was, of course, very solid and I was guessing that they hadn't installed an interior door latch just in case they had made a mistake.

I was about to give up and just surrender to

the cold, black void, when I remembered the new cell phone in my pocket.

It took every bit of strength I had left to pull the phone from my pocket.

I figured I had enough left to make one call.

I punched #2 on the speed dial and Ox' face appeared on the phone.

I was running out of steam and the only thing I could think of was to text the number '8' which I had seen on the chamber door.

I pushed 'send', and hoped that the signal from my phone wouldn't be buried in the vault along with my frozen body.

I had just enough strength for one more push and I hit #1 on the speed dial.

Maggie's smiling face came on the screen and I held the phone where I could see it.

If I was going to bite the big one, the last thing I wanted to remember was my sweetie.

I was about to drift off into oblivion when I heard muffled voices.

"He's got to be in here somewhere! The GPS pinpointed this location."

Then I heard Ox's voice. "Eight! He's texted the number '8'!"

"There!" another voice said. "Vault number eight. That has to be it."

I heard footsteps and then the metallic clunk of the door latch.

The door swung open, light and warmth flooded the chamber and I saw the smiling face of my partner.

Ox and Willie helped me from the cold slab and some guy from the morgue wrapped me in blankets and brought me a cup of hot coffee.

At first, I was too cold to speak.

"You can thank your old pal here for saving your hide," Ox said. "Willie saw them load you into the ambulance and drive away.

"He called me and I had our tekkie guys track you with the GPS in your new phone --- and --- well --- here we are."

By this time, the feeling was beginning to return to my extremities and I could finally speak.

"It's the EMT from the Dr. Death crimes scenes. He's got a buddy and I know where they're going --- but we've got to hurry!"

"You're not in any shape to go anywhere," Ox said.

"The hell I'm not. Just give me a minute. Those guys tried to ice me and I'll be damned if I'm going to miss the opportunity to take them down."

With the warmth returning to my body, I had the sudden need to urinate.

"Where's the can?" I said. "I need to drain the lizard."

"Well, at least your sense of humor didn't freeze," the morgue guy said, pointing down the hall.

I made it to the stall just in time.

I was enjoying the pause that refreshes when I happened to look down.

"Holy crap!"

My stream, which is normally the golden hues of Mountain Dew, now more closely resembled Welch's Grape Juice.

Then I remembered what the coroner had said about the liquid under Fredrick Manning's chair.

They must have injected me with methocarbamol, and thankfully, it was a temporary condition.

"Good thing," I thought.

Maggie is always complaining about the yellow stains in my under shorts.

She asked me once if I was incontinent and needed to start wearing Depends.

I pointed out to her that this was simply one of the idiosyncrasies of the male anatomy and quoted her the verse.

"No matter how you jiggle or how you dance,
The last two drops are in your pants."

She didn't buy it.

I wasn't sure how I was going to explain the two black smudges on my fly.

After a quick conversation with the captain, we headed to the old Randolph Hotel on Main Street where we were to meet up with guys from the tactical unit.

Once we had determined the location of the perps, the troops would storm the castle and our copycat killers would be behind bars.

The old Randolph was a relic from back in the twenties.

It was probably a fine old hotel in its day, but you could see at first glance that it was about ready for the wrecking ball.

It made the Three Trails look like the Ritz.

We met the tactical guys.

The team leader said that the EMT had been identified as a Warren Meeker.

When the team, in full combat gear, flooded the lobby, the night clerk behind the desk nearly dropped a load in his pants.

"Warren Meeker! What room! NOW!" the leader barked.

The quivering clerk looked at his roster. "N-n-n-number 612. Top floor."

Two guys took the rickety elevator and two more took the stairs.

Ox and I followed up the stairs.

We actually reached the sixth floor before the elevator arrived.

We huddled outside of 612. The leader gave a nod and one of the guys smashed the battering ram into the door.

Wood splintered and the team rushed in shouting, "POLICE! ON THE GROUND! NOW!"

I entered and saw a guy on his knees with his hands behind his head.

"That's not Meeker," I said. "That's his accomplice."

"WHERE'S MEEKER?" the leader shouted.

The man just stared straight ahead with an insolent look on his face.

One of the team came into the room.

"Boss. There's a hole in the bathroom wall. It goes into room 610 next door. He must have gone through there."

"Quick! Into the hall. Break into 610. Cover

the exits."

I went to the window and looked into the back alley.

A figure had climbed out the window of room 610 and was going down the fire escape.

"He's out here!" I yelled. "Cut him off at both ends of the alley."

I looked at the old fire escape just outside the window of room 612.

It was made of cast iron that had nearly rusted through from ninety years of exposure to the elements.

It was held to the wall by big lug nuts screwed into the crumbling mortar between the bricks.

Meeker was almost to the ground and I didn't know if the tactical unit could seal the alley before he escaped.

I stepped out onto the rungs of the old ladder and it groaned under my weight.

I started climbing down, the rust crumbling between my fingers.

Miraculously, the thing held and I found myself on the third floor landing.

It was a thirty-foot drop to the ground!

"What kind of fire escape stops at the third floor?" I wondered.

Then I saw it.

It was one of those old escapes I had seen in the movies where a sliding metal ladder drops you the final two stories to the ground.

I could only guess how many years it had been since anyone had tried to use it.

I looked and Meeker had just reached the ground and was heading my direction.

"What the hell," I thought and grabbed the rusty ladder.

The thing groaned, then released and I shot down the last two stories just as Meeker passed beneath.

The ladder hit the ground with a 'thud' about three feet in front of the sprinting Meeker.

His momentum carried him full force into the ladder, knocking him to the ground.

I pounced on top of him and pinned his arms behind his back.

He looked around and seeing it was me, said, "I ---I thought you were dead."

I smiled and whacked him on the back of his head.

"The reports of my death are greatly exaggerated."

I smacked him again.

"Mark Twain said that, you asshole."

158

CHAPTER 12

Things were finally on an even keel.

Dad was no worse for wear from is near abduction, the copycat killers were behind bars and my pee was back to bright yellow again.

As the captain had predicted, it seemed that Dr. Death had taken a hiatus.

No more mercy killings had turned up and we were no closer to catching Thanatos than we were before the undercover operation.

I, for one, welcomed the respite.

After being nearly flash frozen and buried alive, I needed a break.

I had discovered that my sixty-eight year old body didn't bounce back as quick as it used to.

I had taken a few days off to recuperate and was enjoying an evening reading with my sweetie, when there was a knock on the door.

I assumed it was Willie or Jerry, but when I opened the door, a total stranger stood before me.

"Are you Walter Williams?" he asked.

"Yes, I am. Is there something I can help you with?"

"I hope so," he replied. "My name is Mark Davenport. I'm your brother!"

My mouth dropped open.

"Excuse me?"

At that moment, Maggie came up beside me.

"Then you must be Maggie," Davenport said.

Maggie looked at me questioningly.

He introduced himself again.

"Maggie, my name is Mark Davenport and I'm Walt's brother."

This time, Maggie's jaw dropped.

"I know this probably comes as a shock," Davenport said, "but if I could have a minute of your time, I'll explain."

Maggie recovered before I did.

"Walt, maybe you should invite Mr. Davenport inside."

"Call me Mark, please."

I stood aside and Davenport followed Maggie

to the living room.

When we were seated, Davenport spoke first.

"I know this is awkward and I wouldn't have come but --- there are --- extenuating circumstances."

"Before we get to 'circumstances'," I said, "how about telling me what makes you think that I'm your brother."

"Actually, half-brother," he replied. "As you know, your dad was a trucker."

I knew where this was going.

My dad had been an over-the-road trucker and was rarely home.

He had a reputation for being a womanizer.

It was the fifties and my poor mother had looked the other way instead of divorcing the lothario and bringing shame onto the family.

After Mom died, my dad and I drifted apart and I hadn't seen him in years until a year and a half ago when he was kicked out of an Arizona assisted living facility for boinking too many of the old ladies.

I hadn't wanted to take him in, but as it turned out, the old guy had come to his senses and settled down.

Now he was only boinking one woman, my tenant, Bernice.

"Look," I said. "If this is about my dad, I think he should be here."

161

"Well, what I came to talk to you about doesn't concern your father."

"There's a man sitting in my living room telling me that my father sired a child out of wedlock. Yea, I think he needs to be part of this conversation."

"As you wish," he said.

I picked up the phone.

"Dad, can you come up for a minute? ----- No, I don't think it would be a good idea to bring Bernice."

We sat in stony silence until Dad entered the room.

Davenport rose and extended his hand.

"Mr. Williams, my name is Mark Davenport."

"Call me, John," Dad said, shaking his hand. "Davenport ---- I used to know a Davenport."

"I don't suppose it would have been Sarah?" he asked. "Sarah Davenport."

Dad looked at the man closely. "Yes, Sarah. You have her eyes. Are you her son?"

"Yes, Dad," I said. "Mark is her son, and according to him, yours too."

Dad's knees buckled and I had to help him to a chair.

"How --- why ---?" was all he could mutter.

"Why didn't she tell you that she was pregnant?" he asked. "Because you were married and

162

had a ten year old son," he said, looking at me.

By this time Dad had recovered some.

He looked at each of us.

"I was driving the Colorado route. Goodland, Kansas was about halfway. I would always stop at the Blue Moon cafe. That's where I met Sarah.

"Goodland was this little burg out in the middle of nowhere. I was lonely, being on the road all of the time, and I guess Sarah was lonely too.

"At first, we just talked, but after a while, it became more. I would stop every time I passed through Goodland."

He looked directly at Mark. "I never led her on. I told her right up front that I was married and had a kid."

"I know you did," Mark said. "She told me."

"Then the company changed my route and I was going east. I never saw her again. What's it been --- fifty years?"

"Fifty-eight," Mark said.

"So why are you here now," I asked, "after all these years?"

"It's about Mom," he said.

"How is she?" Dad asked.

"She's dying. That's why I'm here."

"Oh my God," Dad said, burying his face in his hands.

Davenport turned to me.

"I've been following your Dr. Death case very closely."

"You mean through the newspapers?"

"No, actually, more than that. I know pretty much every detail about your undercover operation. I'm with the FBI."

"You're a Fed? What's the FBI's interest in our case."

"They're not. I'm interested. It's personal."

"Personal, how?"

"Mom's been sick for a very long time. Pancreatic cancer. It's spread throughout her body. She's done the chemo and the radiation, but there's nothing more they can do for her."

"I'm really sorry to hear that. What does that have to do with our case?"

Then it dawned on me.

"No! No! You surely aren't expecting me to hook you up with Dr. Death?"

"Walt, she's in terrible pain. She's begging to die."

The specter of the dying patients in the Kevorkian movie filled my mind.

"Mark, you know this is illegal. How do I know you're not just testing me? It wouldn't be the first sting I've seen."

"Walt, we don't know each other, but we're still flesh and blood. I wouldn't be here if I didn't love her so much.

"She's had a rough life, raising a kid all alone. She deserves to have her peace and leave this life with some dignity."

Everyone was looking at me.

"But I'm a cop!" I said. "I'm supposed to be trying to catch this guy, not give him more business."

Maggie took my hand.

"I understand what you're going through here, Walt. Nobody's going to try to make you do something you don't feel comfortable with," she said looking first at Dad and then at Mark. "You do what you feel is right in your heart."

I remembered the chat I had with Pastor Bob. His last words that night were, "We have been given guidelines as to what is right and wrong, but circumstances alter cases, and all we can do is make the best choice possible at the time."

I got a pencil and paper and wrote one name, Dr. Graves.

Davenport stuffed the paper in his pocket, hugged me and said, "You have no idea how much this means to me."

As he walked out of the room, my only thought was, *"God help me if I'm wrong."*

165

CHAPTER 13

A few days later, the captain called Ox and me into his office.

I was surprised to see Agent Blackburn with the FBI.

"Oh crap," I thought, *"they've found out about the information that I leaked to Mark Davenport."*

Apparently that was not the case, as Blackburn rose from his chair and extended his hand.

"Well if it isn't Henry Gondorff," he said with a smile. "Good to see you again."

Henry Gondorff was the name I had recently used in a joint undercover operation with the FBI.

We had set up a sting to expose the corruption that existed between large pharmaceutical giants and government officials.

The sting had been a success, but the corporate executives, congressmen and bureaucrats involved had walked away with a mere slap on the wrist.

The end result was a blatant miscarriage of justice, but it had served as a wakeup call that our lives were being manipulated by the collusion of big business and government officials on the take.

"How may I be of service to the FBI today?" I asked.

Blackburn gave me a mischievous grin. "Is my aged David ready to take on another Goliath?"

I was still mad as hell that people of power and influence were somehow able to break the law with impunity and walk away scot-free.

"I might be," I replied. "What do you have in mind?"

"First of all," he said, "I want you to know that not everyone in government is corrupt."

"You could have fooled me," I replied. "Present company excepted, of course."

"Our little sting operation got the attention of some folks in the Department of Justice who are not beneficiaries of the pharmaceutical company's largesse.

"They had been concerned for some time about what they call 'selective enforcement' by some of our government agencies.

"The Rolotor drug fiasco that we exposed focused the spotlight on one of the worst offenders, the Food and Drug Administration."

"If your new operation has anything to do with weeding out the corruption in the FDA, then I'm in," I said. Then looking at the captain, "That is, if it's all right with Captain Short."

The captain smiled. "I think we can spare you and Ox for awhile for a good cause.

"Dr. Death seems to be off the radar for the moment and unless he resurfaces, we'd be happy to loan you to the FBI."

I felt pretty sure that we wouldn't be hearing from Thanatos in the next few days. He was probably on his way to Goodland, Kansas.

"So how can we help?" I asked.

"I'm sure you recall that the FDA has the authority to create a law, and one of their most absurd, states that only a drug can cure, prevent or treat a disease."

I remembered all right.

In Kevin Trudeau's book, *Natural Cures "They" Don't Want You To Know About"*, he gave an example of the absurdity of this 'law'.

He said that the disease of scurvy, which is a vitamin C deficiency, could be treated, prevented and

168

cured by eating citrus fruit.

He went on to say that if a person were to hold up an orange and declare that it was a cure for scurvy, that orange would suddenly become a drug under their definition and the person making that claim could be arrested for selling a drug without a license.

His claim was that the FDA used this tactic, in collusion with the big drug companies to keep natural products off the market, thereby giving the drug giants a monopoly with their expensive, patented drugs.

Blackburn brought me back to the present.

"One of the classic cases of 'selective enforcement' occurred in the late seventies.

"Through extensive research, a man and his wife developed a bread product, made of all-natural ingredients, that had the ability to curb hunger.

"Testing showed that it was effective in weight loss and that the natural fiber contained in the bread could potentially lower the risk of certain cancers.

"This, of course, drew the attention of the drug giants who set loose their minions in the FDA.

"It was a tragic case. The poor man did everything possible to comply with the FDA's requirements for a new food product, but they

169

declared it to be a drug. It wasn't a drug. It was bread! But by their definition, he was selling a drug without a license.

"The guy fought tooth and nail, but in the end, the FDA had all the bread seized. There was enough bread to feed nearly a million people, but rather than give it away, they had it buried in a landfill. Bread!

"The fiasco included collusion beginning with the local FDA office, through congress and all the way to the White House. National television stations and major newspapers were involved as well.

"The man fought so hard that a friend of his who had inside information, told him that if he didn't back off, his family could be the target of an assassination attempt."

I could certainly believe that.

Our sting operation had linked at least seven deaths to the Rolotor drug cover-up.

"Truly a David versus Goliath story, for sure," I said. "So what is David going to have in his sling to take down the giants this time?"

"Elderberries," he replied.

"You've got to be kidding!"

"Nope," he replied. "Elderberries are our perfect weapons.

"Their medicinal properties have been known as far back as Hippocrates.

"They are high in vitamins A, B and C and they have a high concentration of a thing called anthocyanin, one of the most powerful antioxidants known to man.

"Among its other uses is the ability to lower the risk of cardiovascular disease by reducing the oxidation of LDL cholesterol in the blood --- and you know how uptight the drug companies get when you try to introduce a natural product that competes with their statin drugs."

"So how do Ox and I fit into this picture?"

"You're going to help us get the Bob Gordon Elderberry."

I had to think where I had heard that name, and then it came to me.

Bob Gordon and his wife, Kay, were the proprietors of Gordon's Orchard in Osceola, Mo.

Maggie and I had met them when we stopped at the orchard on the way to Branson.

Then a year or so later, another case involving religious extremists had taken me to Osceola during which time we made several more trips to the orchard for their succulent peaches and tomatoes.

"So what does Bob Gordon have to do with elderberries?" I asked.

"The University of Missouri Extension was collecting samples of elderberry germplasm to test. In

1999, Bob Gordon submitted cuttings of the berries growing wild on his land. After extensive research, his berry was selected by the University as the prototype they wanted, and they named it the 'Bob Gordon Elderberry'.

"I'm still not getting the connection," I said.

"It's the perfect setup!" Blackburn said. "Gordon has the elderberry named after him and he has a thriving market.

"We want to set him up with the equipment to process the berries into juice which he will sell in his market with a label that promotes the healing qualities of the juice.

"We'll run ads for the stuff that will get the attention of the drug companies.

"When they unleash their FDA dogs, we'll round up the whole bunch."

"So all I have to do is convince a seventy-year old couple to spit in the face of the federal government and the pharmaceutical giants?"

"Something like that. We'll have their back all the way."

"Yea, I'm sure that will be a comfort."

As Ox and I drove the two hours from Kansas City to Osceola, I tried my best to come up with a reasonable argument to persuade the Gordon's to participate in Blackburn's hair-brained scheme --- but I came up empty.

How do you convince someone to put something they had built over thirty-five years on the line, especially when the outcome was unpredictable?

I had dug into the bread story that Blackburn had shared and I discovered that the FDA had completely ruined the guy and cost him tens of thousands in legal fees.

It wasn't exactly a persuasive argument.

We decided that the best approach was to just be honest, lay everything on the line and see what happened.

When we walked into the market, Bob was behind the counter wearing the same old leather hat I had seen three years ago.

"Hi Mr. Gordon," I said. "Do you remember me?"

"Sure," he said. You're that cop fella from Kansas City. You're too late for the peaches, but we've got lots of apples."

"Actually, we're not here just for the fruit. This is my partner, George Wilson. I wonder if we

173

could have a few minutes with you and your wife?"

"Come on over to the house. I think Kay just took a pie out of the oven."

Bob invited us to sit around the big oak table in the kitchen while Kay was busy spooning big slabs of hot apple pie onto plates.

While we ate, I explained the reason for our visit.

Bob sat quietly until I was finished.

"I see a few problems here," he said. "First, I don't have the equipment to extract the juice from the elderberry and second, even if I did, I don't have enough berries to make the quantities you're talking about."

"The FBI has that all covered," Ox said. "They will install the berry presses and they have made arrangements for berries to be shipped in.

"The bottles are even ready with the labels."

"According to the story you told us about the man with the bread," Kay said, "the FDA could come in at any time and shut down the whole market and we could even be open to criminal charges."

"We hope that is exactly what will happen. We want the FDA to raid the market, but as far as any criminal charges, you will have complete immunity and the DOJ will reimburse you for any lost business."

"And for your co-operation," Ox added, "you can keep the juice presses and any profits from juice sales that come in before the raid."

"Plus," I said, "you get two extra laborers for free. Ox and I will be here to oversee the project to the end. The FBI is putting us up in a hotel in Clinton, so we will be just a half-hour away."

"I don't suppose we could get all that in writing?" Bob asked.

"Got it right here," I said, pulling a sheaf of documents out of my briefcase.

"You all have another piece of pie while Kay and I talk," he said.

I politely declined, but Ox gladly accepted another piece and dug in.

He had just put the last bite in his mouth when the Gordon's returned.

"We've been at this for thirty-five years," he said. "We've been thinking of selling and letting some younger folks try their hand.

"Maybe this is the answer we've been looking for. If we're gonna go out, we might as well go out with a bang!"

It was settled.

A sixty-eight year old cop and two seventy-year old farmers were about to grab another pharmaceutical tiger by the tail.

175

The setup ran like clockwork.

The berry presses were installed, boxes of bottles with the incriminating labels arrived, and soon refrigerated trucks began unloading crates of elderberry heads.

While all this was going on, Ox and I were given a crash course in the orchard business.

We took turns in the field picking apples and Bob even let me drive the tractor.

I hadn't driven a tractor since I was a boy on my grandpa's farm. I was like a kid in a candy store.

But the thing that I wanted to do the most was drive the forklift. Since my high school days as a stock boy at the local supermarket, the powerful machines that lifted the huge pallets of groceries had fascinated me. The lift was, of course, off limits to a sixteen year-old kid.

At the orchard, the apples were brought in from the field in huge wooden crates weighing hundreds of pounds.

176

The forklift would carry the crates into an enormous walk-in cooler where they were stacked to the ceiling.

With some misgivings, Bob instructed me in the use of the lift.

The first time I tried it on my own, I saw Bob watching and his hands were behind his back. I'm guessing he had his fingers crossed.

Once the elderberry operation was underway, Ox and I learned to operate the press.

We discovered right away that another characteristic of the juice is that it stains --- horribly!

After my first day in the pressroom, I emerged looking more like Willie than Walt.

The bumblings of Ox and I that first day, brought back memories of that *I Love Lucy* classic where Lucy and Ethel were in the big vat stomping grapes barefooted.

Thankfully, we weren't required to take off our shoes.

It wasn't long before the first bottles of elderberry elixir were ready to sell.

As promised, the Fibbies ran full-page ads in the Clinton, Springfield and Kansas City newspapers extolling the virtues of the juice as a way to control cholesterol levels naturally, with no damaging side effects at a fraction of the cost of statin drugs.

177

The day the newspapers hit the streets, the phones began to ring and cars began pouring into the market parking lot.

We sold out of our first batch in two days and worked late into the night to prepare more of the sought-after juice.

Sales skyrocketed, and for the moment, the Gordon's were pleased with their decision.

The bulk of the sales were for cash and Kay found herself making daily trips to the bank.

About ten days into the operation, Bob approached us waving a letter in his hand.

"I think you've got someone's attention," he said, handing us the letter.

The letter was exactly what we had anticipated.

DEPARTMENT OF HEALTH EDUCATION AND WELFARE

Mr. Robert Gordon
Osceola, Mo.

Dear Mr. Gordon,

Our investigation has revealed that you have been marketing Gordon's Elderberry Elixir with the label bearing a claim that your product will reduce

178

the oxidation of LDL cholesterol in the blood thereby preventing cardiovascular disease.

Such claims and statements cause this elixir to be a new drug. A new drug cannot be marketed until the Food and Drug Administration has received and approved a New Drug Application (NDA) for the product.

In summary, it is the opinion of the Food and Drug Administration that Gordon's Elderberry Elixir is a new drug and as labeled is seriously misbranded and, therefore, may not be marketed with its present labeling in the absence of an approved new Drug Application.

In view of the above and in the public interest, we request that you immediately discontinue marketing Gordon's Elderberry Elixir as labeled and immediately discontinue all distribution of promotional literature.

We request that you reply within ten (10) days after receipt of this letter, stating the action you will take to discontinue the marketing of this drug product. If such corrective action is not promptly undertaken, the Food and Drug Administration is prepared to initiate legal action to enforce the law.

The Federal Food, Drug and Cosmetic Act provides for seizure of illegal products and/or injunction against the manufacturer or distributor of *illegal product, 21 U.S.C. 332 and 334.*

Sincerely,
Reginald Baldwin
District Director

Bingo!

This was what we had been waiting for.

"So what do we do now?" Bob asked. "Remember, I'm too old to go to jail!"

I assured him that nothing was going to happen, but if it did, we would try to arrange for he and Kay to have adjoining cells.

He didn't find that amusing.

I faxed the letter to Agent Blackburn and advised him to circle the wagons because the savages were just over the hill.

He liked my old west metaphor.

The ads continued to run and the customers continued pouring in.

We should have anticipated that the extra cash in the daily till would attract the attention of some unsavory individuals, but our attention was so fixed on the white-collar crooks, we weren't prepared for villains of the blue-collar variety.

One afternoon, just before closing, the gal that ran the register was filling the bank bag when a scruffy guy with a full beard and his hair pulled back in a pony-tail approached the counter.

Ox and I had just finished cleaning the elderberry press and were looking forward to a meal of country bar-b-que.

We rounded the corner just in time to see Mr. Ponytail level a gun at the clerk and point to the cash bag.

We ducked back before the guy saw us.

Our weapons were, of course, locked in our car.

Farm hands typically don't carry side arms, even in Osceola.

"We can't rush him," Ox said. "There's a good fifty feet of open space. He could get off two shots easily before we get to him."

Then I saw it.

"I've got an idea," I said. "You go out the back, circle around and wait for him just outside the door. I'll flush him out and you can take him down."

"So how will this flush thing work?" Ox asked.

I pointed to the forklift.

"An apple a day, keeps the scumbag at bay."

He nodded and took off.

I climbed into the forklift, fired it up and loaded one of the huge crates of apples.

I was hoping that the two wooden sides of the crate plus the four feet of apples would be of sufficient density to stop a slug.

I'd soon find out.

I rounded the corner, got my bearings and just as the thug raised his gun toward me, lifted the apples to block the trajectory of the bullets.

I heard the sound of the six shots and felt the impact as the slugs buried deep into my Honey Crisp armor.

The creep, being out of ammo and seeing the lift bearing down on him, turned and fled out the door, running headlong into a mountain of flesh.

It only took one swing of Ox's meaty fist to drop the jerk to his knees.

The sound of the shots drew Bob and Kay from their home.

Bob looked at the perp lying on the ground and then his attention focused on the crate dripping juice from the dozens of apples that had been perforated by the slugs.

His only comment was, "You city boys sure have a strange way of making cider."

It was business as usual for the next few days.

Then I received a call from Blackburn. He said that his informants had told him that the raid was imminent.

I hoped so.

I had been away from Maggie way too long.

She would drive down for an evening and we would have supper together, but it just wasn't the same.

I had just finished an undercover stint as a dead man in the Dr. Death sting that had taken me away from home and now with this, I had been away from her for almost a month.

I had grown quite fond of Kay's apple pie, but it just couldn't take the place of Maggie's sweet kisses.

The day began like any other; the frost on the pumpkin melting away under the bright morning sun.

About ten o'clock someone pointed to Highway Thirteen.

Coming from the north was a line of cars that, at first glance, appeared to be a funeral procession.

A closer look revealed that the vehicles were big black SUV's and not stretch limos.

"This is it," I said. "Let's prepare a special welcome for our guests."

We knew that the purpose of the raid was to seize all of the bottles, juice and berries and put Gordon's Elixir out of business just as they had done with the bread company.

Bread was one thing, but sticky elderberry juice, the consistency of India ink was quite another.

We had figured out how to rig the storage vats holding the juice so that an unsuspecting interloper would have a rude surprise.

The SUV's rolled into the parking lot with red and blue lights flashing from under their grills.

They poured out of the cars with guns drawn and swarmed the market.

184

"U.S. Marshals! Everyone stay where you are and put your hands in the air!"

All of the market employees had known what was coming, but the half-dozen customers who had been milling about, stood frozen with fear.

The whole scene was reminiscent of the old movies depicting the Nazi Gestapo raiding a village looking for Jews in hiding.

Quickly, the guy in charge separated the employees from the customers.

He herded the employees into a corner and ordered us to stay put.

He grabbed bottles of elderberry juice from the shaking hands of terrified customers and ushered them out the door.

When all that was left was market employees, he addressed the group.

"Which one of you is Robert Gordon?"

Bob raised his hand and stepped forward.

The marshal handed Bob an official-looking document.

"This is an order from the Food and Drug Administration authorizing us to seize everything associated with the production and sale of Gordon's Elderberry Elixir."

"Have at it," Bob said with a smile.

The marshals backed a truck up to the door of

the market and began loading the bottles of juice from the display shelf.

When they had finished, they asked Bob for the bottles waiting to be filled.

He showed them where they were located in the storage area and the marshals loaded that too.

With that job completed, the guy in charge approached Bob again.

"Is there anything else on the premises associated with the illegal drug?"

"Well, if you're talking about my juice," he replied, "there's a whole vat of it back in the cooler that we were about to put in bottles."

The guy motioned for one of his underlings to check out the juice.

"What am I supposed to do with a vat of juice?" the underling asked.

"Our orders say to remove EVERYTHING associated with the drug, so figure it out!"

"Yes, Sir."

The man disappeared into the cooler and in just a few minutes we heard ---

"OH SHIT!"

At that moment, another procession of SUV's stormed into the parking lot.

Blackburn hopped out of the car followed by small army of guys in FBI jackets.

"I'm Agent Blackburn with the FBI," he said, handing the marshal an official-looking paper.

"This is an order signed by the Attorney General ordering you to stand down. Please surrender your weapons and your car keys. We're taking you into custody."

The marshal handed Blackburn his weapon just as the underling emerged from the cooler covered from head-to-toe with black sticky goo.

Blackburn gave me a grin and said, "Well, Br'er Bear. Looks like we got us a tar baby."

We wrapped up the elderberry caper and headed home.

The Gordon's got to keep the berry press as promised and the Feds even gave them new bottles with labels more in tune with the current law.

Plus, he had raked in a bundle from the sale of the new juice.

The word spread rapidly that the Bob and Kay were part of an FBI undercover operation and they soon became local heroes.

On the day we parted company, Kay gave Ox a pie fresh out of the oven and Bob handed me a peck of apples.

"Got you some without bullet holes," he said, smiling.

Blackburn kept me informed about the progress of our sting.

The marshals, it turned out, were simply unsuspecting pawns in the 'selective enforcement' scheme.

Their orders had come from the Kansas City office of the FDA.

The order had been passed down to them directly from the FDA's Center for Drug Evaluation and Research.

The Center's director, coincidently, had a son on the board of directors of Martin Pharmaceuticals.

One of their most profitable drugs just happened to be a statin whose purpose was to regulate cholesterol.

Based on our work, the Attorney General launched an investigation into the regulatory practices of the FDA and its relationship with the large drug companies.

While our little victory couldn't be classified as a knockout punch, it was a start.

Undoubtedly there would be stonewalling and arm twisting, and congressmen and bureaucrats who had been on the take would be getting calls from the CEO's of the drug giants calling in their favors.

Years could pass before there would be any real reform in the system that had become so badly corrupted, but if it happened in my lifetime, I would be proud to say that I had a small part in it.

I had been in Osceola for the better part of two weeks and on my return, my friends and family insisted on throwing a party.

I appreciated the gesture, but my goal was some alone time with Maggie.

I enjoyed the laughing and the jokes and the food, but I was relieved when the last guest departed.

189

Maggie smiled and gave me her 'come hither' look.

I didn't have to be asked twice.

We had some 'catching up' to do.

I just didn't realize that we were going to do all our 'catching up' in one night!

A cop's schedule can be frustrating, but a realtor's can be just as bad.

A good agent must work when their clients are available.

Maggie had been working with a gal whose husband was being transferred into Kansas City.

They had pre-selected several homes in anticipation of his arrival.

His plane had landed and he was anxious to see the homes that evening.

Maggie called and said that she would just grab a quick bite on the run and that I was on my own for supper.

While I would miss my sweetie, I realized that this wasn't all together a terrible thing.

Maggie had succeeded in steering my diet from fried things to grilled things and from tasty starches to green things.

I was slowly being morphed from a carnivore to a herbivore, but old habits die slowly.

I figured that this was my night to pay Mel a visit.

Prior to my nuptials, Mel's Diner was my eatery of choice.

Most everything on his menu was either deep-fried or fried on the grill in butter.

I decided on a chicken-fried steak with fluffy potatoes, all smothered in greasy gravy. Of course it came with a huge slice of Texas toast, buttered and grilled.

I topped it all off with a generous slice of lemon pie with meringue three inches high.

I figured that I would have to graze on greens for a month to make up for my debauchery.

I left the diner so full I could barely waddle.

I was on the way to my car when two men came up beside me.

I felt something being pressed into my side and guessed that it wasn't the guy's finger.

"Just keep walking," the guy said. "We're going to that black van just ahead."

When we reached the van, one guy opened

191

the cargo door while the other one patted me down.

I had left my gun in my car before going into Mel's. I suppose it was just as well. They'd have just taken it anyway.

After determining that I was unarmed, he gave me a shove. "Get in."

One guy hopped into the driver's seat and the other sat on a bench opposite me with a gun trained at my chest.

"Who are you guys?" I asked.

"I guess it really doesn't matter if I tell you since you won't be in a position to tell anyone else."

That wasn't a message that I wanted to hear.

"Apparently you've pissed off some very powerful people," he said. "The marks that my partner and I usually get are drug lords, crime bosses or other assassins. We've never been hired to do an old cop.

"They don't give us details, but I hear you've been stepping on the toes of some drug company bigwigs with political connections.

"That'll get you killed, you know."

"Can we talk about this?" I asked.

He looked at his watch. "You can talk all you want for the next ten minutes, cause after that, you won't be talking no more."

I realized that bargaining with a hired assassin

was a waste of what little breath I had left.

I burped and got a second taste of the lemon pie.

"Well," I thought, *"at least my last meal was a dandy."*

"Exactly how do you plan to do this?" I asked.

Then I remembered the old guy on the front porch of the Three Trails who said that if he knew where he was going to die, he simply wouldn't go there.

I didn't think that was going to be an option under these circumstances.

"We're professionals," he said. "No guns or knives --- too messy and they leave too many clues. You're going to have a terrible accident."

I looked out the window and saw that we were in downtown Kansas City.

The van turned into a parking garage and began to slowly wind up the ramps to the top floor.

I counted six levels before we reached the roof.

The driver parked and opened the cargo door.

"Out!" he barked.

They each grabbed an arm and drug me to the roof railing.

I looked over the edge. It was a long, long

way down and I was afraid of heights to begin with.

I had heard of cruel twists of fate where guys who were afraid of water drowned and here I was, an acrophobic who was about to be tossed over the edge.

"Any last words?" the guy asked.

I turned to speak, but instead of words coming out of my mouth, it was Mel's delicious dinner.

Lemon pie, Texas toast, chicken fried steak and fluffy potatoes all smothered in gravy erupted and covered the guy from head to toe.

"Arrrrrrrrghhhhh," he shouted.

The next thing I knew, I was being hoisted over the guardrail.

I hung suspended for just a moment and a final shove pushed me over the edge.

The last thing I heard was the guy screaming, "Have a nice trip, you puke!"

I had experienced dreams where I was flying. It had been exhilarating. I would launch out and glide over the hills and trees and I always awoke refreshed and comfortable in my bed.

This was nothing like that at all.

I saw the pavement coming at me from six stories below and realized that I wouldn't be waking up in my comfortable bed.

About midway into my swan dive, I saw the red and white umbrella of a tamale cart moving my direction.

At the last moment I realized that the cart and I were on a collision course.

I suddenly realized the irony of the situation. I was going to die on top of a tamale cart and I didn't even like tamales.

CHAPTER 14

When I opened my eyes, I was totally disoriented.

I looked down and there, far below, I saw the body of Walter Williams lying in a hospital bed.

The face was covered with an oxygen mask, bags of liquid were dripping into tubes inserted into the arms and an overhead machine displayed digital readouts of his vital signs.

Maggie was at the bedside holding his hand.

A small circle of friends and family stood quietly in the corner.

The drama being played out below, reminded me of a play in which I acted in high school.

It was called *Balcony Scene*.

I played St. Peter and my best friend, Kenny, played the part of a man who had died.

St. Peter and the man were in the balcony of the funeral home looking down on the service below.

The gist of the story was that St. Peter was giving the man the opportunity to see and hear what his friends and family thought of him, based on the life that he had lived.

Fifty years had passed and I still remembered the two opening lines of the play.

"Are you sure we won't be seen?"
"Yes, I am quite sure."

My first thought was that surely they must know that I am up here --- wherever 'here' might be.

Then I remembered that in the play, the guy was dead, and my second thought was wondering whether I might have cashed in my chips as well.

At that moment, a man in a white coat entered the room. The stethoscope around his neck led me to believe that he was a doctor.

He read the chart attached to the foot of the bed and then studied the digital readouts.

He spoke and I heard every word as clearly as if he were standing right beside me.

"The good news is that his vitals are stable."

"And the bad news?" Maggie asked.

"He is still in a deep coma. With a head injury like he sustained, there is no way of knowing how soon --- or even if, he will wake up."

197

He turned to the little knot of family and friends.

"You all might as well go on home and get some rest. He might regain consciousness in a matter of hours, or it could be days, or maybe never. He's stable for now and we'll call you if there's any change."

Dad came over and put his hand on Maggie's shoulder.

"Come on, honey. You need to get some sleep."

"I can't leave him," she replied. "You all go. I'll let you know if anything changes."

Each one, in turn, gave Maggie a hug, and a pat on the hand to the body in the bed.

After they were gone, Maggie laid her head on the side of the bed, never letting go of the limp hand.

I suddenly became aware of the presence of a bright light that grew in intensity.

I turned toward the light and saw a figure approaching out of its brilliance.

At first, I couldn't distinguish the features of the apparition, but when it spoke, I recognized the voice.

"She's quite a gal, isn't she Walter?"

Then, the voice and the figure blended into

one.

"Mom! Is that you?"

"Yes, Walter. It's your mother."

I moved forward to embrace her, but she held up her hand.

"Sorry, son, but at this time, think of our meeting like when you were undercover as a 'john' at the Red Garter --- looky but no touchy."

"You know about that?"

"Of course I know. You're my son."

"So you're coming to me from --- where --- heaven?"

"Sure, let's call it that."

I had read about people who had died and were met by loved ones who led them into the light.

"So are you here to get me? Am I dying?"

"My goodness no. It's not your time yet."

"So what's it like --- up there --- over there --- I'm not quite sure of the terminology."

"I know it's confusing. Just try to think of it as an altered state of consciousness."

"Yea, that certainly clears everything up. But what's it like?"

"Unfortunately, this is a lot like the CIA. I could tell you, but then I'd have to kill you ---- just kidding!"

I didn't remember Mom having such a

warped sense of humor. Maybe that's where I got it.

"So what happened to me?"

"You don't remember being pitched off the roof of the parking garage by a couple of goons?"

"Of course I do. I was falling and --- and then there was that damn tamale cart."

"First of all, please watch your language," she said, looking over her shoulder. "Someone might be listening."

"So there really is a Big Guy?"

"Let's just say that there's an awful lot of stuff going on up here and somebody has to organize it."

"So if there's a heaven, is there a hell as well?"

"Oh, there's definitely a hell. I had to sit through a Taylor Swift concert the other night."

I guessed that hell was different things to different people.

"So let's get back to what happened to me."

"Oh, right. The tamale cart! You have no idea how much trouble it was to get that cart under you at exactly the right moment. The tamale vendor was ogling some chick and we had to employ some desperate measures."

"We? You said 'we'?"

"Sure, your grandfather and me."

"Grandpa is involved in all this stuff too?"

"Well sure. I used to be able to handle most everything, but since you got that wild hair to become a cop, I needed some extra help."

"Where is Grandpa? Can I see him?"

"No, not this time, but someday for sure."

"So you needed extra help --- doing what exactly?"

"Keeping your scrawny butt out of a sling. You keep getting in all those scrapes. Somebody has to pull your fat out of the fire."

I tried to ignore her mixed metaphors.

"What scrapes are you talking about?"

"Well, just the other day, you were about to be flash frozen in the morgue and as I recall, your last act was to send a cell phone message to Ox. Do you have any idea what your grandpa and I had to go through to get you enough bars to get that signal out of that freezer in the basement of that building?"

"You can actually do that?"

"And that's not all. Let's talk about your honeymoon in Hawaii. You just had to scale down a vertical cliff in a volcanic crater. What were you thinking? We worked overtime that day.

"And don't forget the lizards. Do you know how difficult it is to train lizards?"

"So you do animals too?"

201

"Of course. Cats are the worst and, naturally, you had to use a cat to take out the hawk-faced man at Dr. Pearson's house. Have you ever tried herding cats?"

"So it wasn't just a coincidence that I stepped on that cat's tail at just the right moment?"

She smiled. "Son, there's really no such thing as a coincidence."

"So, are you and Grandpa --- like --- angels?"

"Sure, let's call it that."

I wished that she would stop using that phrase.

"We brought you into this world. Just because we croak doesn't mean that our job is over. I'll be your mom forever, no matter how old you are."

It was actually a very comforting thought.

"Oh, when you get back, tell your dad that I said 'hello', and give my best to Bernice."

"You know about Dad and Bernice?"

"Of course I know. Not much gets by us up here."

"And you're OK with it?"

"We look at things from a different perspective. Your dad may have been a crappy husband and father, but he has a good heart.

"I know now that he loved us both and that's what matters."

"So you've forgiven him?"

"That's what we do.

"Oh, and one more thing. Tell Willie that his grandparents are really proud of the exhibit that he donated to the St. Clair County Museum. His family was a big part of the history of that area and now their story will be available for generations to come."

I knew that would please my little friend.

He had never known his grandparents even existed and now to be told that they were proud of him would mean the world to him.

We noticed some movement below. Maggie got up, stretched and sat back down beside the bed.

"You got yourself a good one there, son. What took you so long to pop the question?"

"I guess I just wanted to be sure we were doing the right thing."

"Well, based on what I've seen, you two are doing everything just right."

"Everything? What do you mean by everything? You see EVERYTHING?"

"Well we could. We're interested and we're concerned, but we're not voyeurs."

"Gee, that's a comfort."

Just then, there was a fluxuation in the bright light behind her.

"That's my cue," she said. "Like when they

203

dim the lights at a play just before the curtain goes up. My time is about up."

"So what happens now?" I asked.

"Now it's time to return to your world; time to get back to Maggie."

"You never did tell me what happened when I hit the tamale cart."

"Well, thanks to my perfect timing, you bounced off that umbrella like it was a trampoline. Unfortunately, your dismount wasn't that great.

"You have a couple of cracked ribs, some bruises and you whacked your head on the sidewalk."

I felt my head and ribs.

"How come I don't hurt?"

"Because right now, your spirit is free from the limitations of your earthly body. Trust me, when you go back you're going to hurt.

"Oh, I almost forgot. You've got a job to do."

"Already? I'm still in a coma."

"Not for long. Don't you want to get those two goons who tossed you off the roof?"

"I think I got one of them pretty good already. I seem to recall hurling on him just before he hurled me."

"Yes, that was a nice touch," she said, smiling.

"So what's the job?"

"The goons aren't finished yet. You and Agent Backburn were both thorns in the side of the drug giants. They think they've taken care of you and now they're gunning for Blackburn."

"So what do I do?"

"Just keep your eyes open. You'll know."

The bright light fluxed again.

"Time to go," she said.

"Will I see you again?"

"When the time is right."

"I love you, Mom, and I miss you."

"I love you too, Walt. Always will."

Then she turned and disappeared into the light.

CHAPTER 15

When I opened my eyes again, I was lying in the hospital bed and I was pretty certain that my spirit had reunited with my body, because I hurt like hell.

The memory of my out-of-body experience was still fresh in my mind and the warm feeling that I had from seeing and talking to my mother made the pain more bearable.

I looked around the room for Maggie, but she was not there.

Then I heard the toilet flush and saw her coming toward me.

I tried to speak, but the oxygen mask covering my face muffled the sound.

She sat down beside the bed and when she held my hand, I gave it my best squeeze.

Her eyes met mine and I gave her a wink.

She burst into tears and laid her head on my chest.

"Oh Walt. I thought I'd lost you."

"Mwwuummph," was all I could say from behind the mask.

Maggie pulled the cord attached to the bed and a burly nurse strode into the room.

My first thought was, *Why do all my nurses have to look like Nurse Ratchett?*

"So our boy's awake," she said, flashing a penlight in my eyes.

"How many fingers?" she asked, holding up two.

"Murrromph," I replied.

She lifted the mask off my face.

"Two!"

"How do you feel?"

"Like I just fell six stories from a parking garage. Other than that, fine."

"Sense of humor. Good sign," she said.

She was about to re-mask me.

"Can you please leave that off? I can breathe just fine --- well maybe except for the pain in my ribs."

She checked the monitors.

"Sure."

Having regained full consciousness, I became

aware of a strange sensation in my private parts.

I looked at Maggie. "Mr. Winky! He didn't get crushed, did he?"

"No silly. You have a catheter."

I had heard of those things before and they terrified me.

"How --- who hooked me up?"

Nurse Ratchett smiled a knowing smile. "That would be me."

"Swell," I thought. *"There's no such thing as dignity in a hospital."*

After she had finished probing and poking, the nurse left the room.

"How long have I been here?" I asked.

"This is the second day. I'm so relieved. The doctor wasn't sure that you'd wake up at all."

"You can't get rid of me that easy."

Seeing that I was back among the living, Maggie pulled out her phone.

"I promised everyone that I would call as soon as you woke up. I'm going to make those calls. You just rest."

She made the calls and that initiated a flood of visitors.

Friends, family, cops and even old realtor friends stopped by to wish me well.

Each one, of course, had to bring a flower or a

208

balloon of some sort and before long, my room looked like kid's day at Chuckie Cheese.

The captain was one of my first visitors.

He brought a stenographer to take my statement about the abduction and attempted murder.

When I told him what the thug had said about pissing off some very powerful people in the drug industry, he was furious.

"We have to catch those guys and find out who hired them. Unless we can tie these assassins to one of the executives, they'll just keep coming after our people."

He had mug books delivered to the hospital and I spent hours looking at photos of scumbags, but they just weren't there.

On a lighter note, he pointed out that this was the third tamale cart that the City had to buy for Jim's Famous Tamales.

In addition to the one I had just squashed, another had been blown up during the Gay Pride Parade and I had t-boned a third one while driving a bomb in a trolley car to Loose Park Lake.

On one occasion, Dad had stopped by.

It was just the two of us.

I hadn't told anyone, not even Maggie, about my encounter with my mother, but I figured Dad had the right to know.

"Dad, something very strange occurred while I was in the coma. I saw and spoke to Mom."

"You --- you saw your mother? How?"

"I have no idea how. I just know that I did and she was as real as you are right now."

"Was she --- happy?"

"Yes, very much so, and she asked me to give you a message."

Dad watched me expectantly.

"She wanted you to know that whatever happened between the two of you, she forgives you and she wants you to be happy too. You and Bernice have her blessing."

Dad crumbled.

He put his head in his arms on the side of my bed and wept.

"I never meant to hurt her --- not on purpose. I loved her, but I was just a dumb shit with my head up my ass. I have wished a thousand times that I could do it all over --- for her and for you."

"She wanted to lift that burden off your shoulders and give you peace."

"Thank you," he said. "Thank you both."

I had never really seen the true power of forgiveness, but after watching my dad that day, I figured that maybe the Big Guy had things pretty well under control after all.

The doctor was amazed that an old guy like me could recuperate so quickly.

Maggie, of course, attributed it to my new regimen of healthy food and supplements.

I didn't argue.

Then one morning, after the doctor had looked me over from stem to stern, he declared that I was fit to travel.

I called Maggie and gave her the good news.

She was devastated that she was tied up with clients all day.

I told her not to worry. I would call Ox. He would get me home and I would see her later.

I made the call and was about to change from that disgusting gown into my civvies, when Agent Blackburn walked into the room.

"Hey, Walt. Sorry I haven't been here to see you sooner. The brass has kept me pretty tied up with the elderberry thing. We're making some progress. We've got some of the corporate fat cats and shady politicians shaking in their boots."

"Good to hear," I said. "I suppose you know that they were the ones who had me tossed off the roof."

"I did know that and we've been trying to get a lead on those two, but they've gone underground."

Then I remembered what my mother had said.

211

"You do realize that they're probably after you too."

"As soon as we heard about the attempt on your life, the Bureau assigned teams to watch my back around the clock. There's been no sign of anyone."

"So where are your guys now?" I asked, looking around.

"They're taking a break. We figured I'd be safe in the hospital. They'll pick me up outside."

"Well, you watch your back. I've been released and Ox will be here in a few minutes to take me home."

"Then I'll get out of your hair. As always, it was a pleasure doing business with you. Maybe we can do it again some day."

"Sure. Anytime you need a cadaver, just give me a call."

He laughed and waved and was on his way.

I watched him leave and as soon as he was out of my door, two men in lab coats walked up on either side of him.

I saw one of them press something into his back and whisper in his ear.

The other turned and glanced down the hall.

I saw his face and recognized him as one of the goons who had given me flying lessons.

Blackburn was being abducted and his backup was nowhere in sight.

At that moment Ox walked in the door.

"Hey partner. Are you ready to make like a hockey player and get the puck out of here?"

"Ox," I said pointing, "that's Agent Blackburn and he's being abducted. I think they have a gun in his back."

"OK," he said. "Let's figure this out."

Just then, a portly orderly was wheeling an empty gurney down the hall.

"Quick," I said, "give me your badge and your gun."

Ox handed them over and I flagged down the orderly.

I showed him the badge.

"Kansas City Police. We need your gurney and your scrubs --- NOW!"

The orderly stripped and I tossed the scrubs to Ox.

"Put these on. Quick!"

He slipped on the scrubs and I crawled under the sheet on the gurney.

"This hallway is a big circle. Go the opposite of the way they took Blackburn and we'll cut them off before they reach the elevator. Step on it!"

Ox barreled down the hallway dodging

doctors, patients and nurses.

He swerved around the first corner and almost took out an old guy pushing his saline rack.

We rounded the second corner and saw Blackburn and the two goons heading our way.

As we approached, I sat up on the gurney and caught Blackburn's eye.

He recognized us and nodded.

When we were just a few feet from the trio, I threw back the sheet and leveled Ox's pistol at one of the goons.

"Kansas City Police. Drop your gun and put your hands in the air."

Blackburn did one of those fancy twisty turns that they teach you at Quantico and had the guy with the gun on the floor.

The second guy turned to run, but Ox was on him in a flash.

After they were both in cuffs, one of them gave me a close look.

"I thought you was dead!"

"Yea," I said. "I've been getting that a lot lately. Maybe someday, but not today."

CHAPTER 16

My hospital release was delayed by the debriefing and paperwork involved with the two assassins.

But finally, everything was wrapped up and Ox drove me home.

Everyone in the building wanted to throw another 'Welcome Home Walt' party, but Maggie had persuaded them to give it a rest and let me settle in peacefully.

We enjoyed a leisurely supper and Maggie caught me up on her activities while I had been hospitalized.

Toward the end of the evening, Maggie inquired as to whether my body had recuperated sufficiently to engage in some activities of a more intimate nature.

I did a quick check and determined that I was fit to go.

Maggie slipped into that little black nightie with the fur around the edges that barely covered her --- well, it barely covered it.

My first encounter with this garment was on our honeymoon and Maggie had worn it infrequently since then, usually only on special occasions.

I sensed that she had planned the evening ahead of time and that she considered her husband's return from oblivion, a special occasion.

When we hit the sheets, I could tell that Maggie was ready to go and so was I --- but Mr. Winkie was a no-show.

After a while, Maggie sensed that something was definitely wrong.

"Walt, are you OK. You're usually --- uhhh --- more enthusiastic."

It certainly wasn't a lack of enthusiasm. Maggie had certainly done her best to whet my appetite, but something was holding me back.

Then it occurred to me. I remembered Mom's comment, "Based on what I've seen, you and Maggie are doing everything just right."

It was the 'everything' that had sent Mr. Winkie into hiding.

Somehow a man can't do his best work if he

216

thinks his mom might be in the room watching.

I hadn't told Maggie about my experience while in the coma, and I figured this might be a good time.

I certainly didn't want her to think that my lack of responsiveness reflected on her in any way.

We spent the next hour talking about the visit with my mom.

I have to give Maggie credit. Such a far-fetched story could have been met with skepticism and doubt, but Maggie was totally supportive.

When our discussion of things ethereal had concluded, Maggie looked around the bedroom.

"I have a theory. I'm betting that spirits can't see in the dark any better than we can. Shall we give it a try?"

I turned off the light and crawled into bed next to my sweetie.

In the total darkness of the room, Mr. Winkie suddenly appeared. Maybe Maggie was right.

Later, as I lay back, exhausted, another one of those weird things that inhabit the deep recesses of my brain popped into my mind.

I remembered, as a kid, seeing Jimmy Durante, the comedian, on TV.

After every performance, he would sign off with the words, "Goodnight Mrs. Calabash, wherever you are."

I thought about my mom and how much I missed her and my last words before dropping off to sleep were, "Goodnight Mrs. Williams, wherever you are."

Try as I might, I couldn't get my out-of-body experience out of my mind.

I needed to talk to someone with some insight into things beyond the realm of normal human experience.

My first thought was Pastor Bob, but I already knew what his response would be.

It was a foregone conclusion that he believed in something beyond the decay of our mortal flesh.

It was his Boss who had uttered the words that had brought comfort to the multitudes over the centuries, *"In my Father's house are many mansions. If it were not so, I would have told you. I go to prepare a place for you."*

I had always been willing to go with that, simply because the alternative, that there is nothing more and than we are no different than road kill rotting on the highway, is totally unacceptable.

218

But I wanted a more analytic approach, not based on religious dogma.

The obvious choice was the Professor.

With a Doctorate in Philosophy and years of academic teaching, I thought he might have some valuable insights into my experience.

He listened quietly as I related my incredible story.

When I finished, I simply asked, "Was it real or was I dreaming?"

"I wish that the answer was that simple. The first question on which everything else is based is if there is life after death.

"Life after death can neither be proved nor disproved. This is because one would have to undergo physical death in order to prove or disprove it, and, by its very nature, disproving it would not be possible.

"One either believes or disbelieves and that is the basis of faith."

"Very well then," I said, "let's go with the premise that there is something beyond the grave. How does my experience fit into that scenario?"

"Then it puts you in with a very elite group of individuals. You had what has been called an NDE, a near-death experience, and an OBE, an out-of-body experience. It is estimated that eighteen percent of individuals who had been resuscitated from cardiac arrest have reported the same kind of experience."

"But don't critics explain that away by attributing such phenomena to complex defense mechanisms of a dying brain?"

"That's certainly one explanation. The human brain is the most complex and least understood thing in our known universe.

"As your hero, Dirty Harry, likes to say, 'Opinions are like assholes; everybody has one.' Well brains are like assholes too. Everyone has one, but no one really understands what it is capable of."

"So are you saying that what I experienced was nothing more than screwed up neurons firing away in my cerebral cortex?"

"Quite the contrary. In 1991 in Atlanta, Georgia, Pam Reynolds had a near-death experience. Reynolds underwent surgery for a brain aneurysm, and the procedure required doctors to drain all the blood from her brain. The woman was kept literally brain-dead by the surgical team for a full 45 minutes. Despite being clinically dead, when Reynolds was resuscitated, she described some amazing things. She recounted experiences she had while dead -- like interacting with deceased relatives. Even more amazing is that Reynolds was able to describe aspects of the surgical procedure, down to the bone saw that was used to remove part of her scull."

"So what does that prove?"

"It doesn't 'prove' anything, but a brain-dead person should not be able to form new memories -- he shouldn't have any consciousness at all, really. So how can anything but a metaphysical explanation account for her experience?"

"So are you saying that what I experienced was real?"

"Was it real to you?"

"As real as me sitting here with you right now."

"And how did your experience make you feel?"

"It was one of the most beautiful and comforting experiences in my entire life."

"Then that's all that really matters, isn't it?"

After I left, I realized that the Professor had left me exactly as had Pastor Bob.

I had gone looking for answers.

True or not true?

Real or a figment of my imagination?

But instead, he had made me look deep within, and decide for myself.

I wonder who teaches these guys to do that?

CHAPTER 17

On the day that I returned to work, the captain called Ox and me into his office.

"There has been a new development in the Dr. Death case," he said. "After our undercover operation went sour, we did everything we could to get a lead on the guy.

"There were no fingerprints, so we hit a wall there.

"We tried to strong-arm the four doctors that we suspected of referring patients to the guy, but none of them would talk, and there was no direct evidence tying Thanatos to any of them."

"So what did you come up with?" I asked.

"The only concrete thing we had to go on was the video surveillance footage from the safe house.

"We got some good shots of Thanatos interacting with you, and we ran him through every facial recognition database that we could think of --- but we came up empty.

"Then one day, someone figured out that we were barking up the wrong tree.

"We had been searching databases of known offenders. We started operating on the theory that our guy wasn't a criminal and was, most likely, a doctor."

"So that's how you found him?" Ox asked.

"Yes. We searched dozens of medical databases and found nothing, but then one of the tekkies found an obscure database of doctors who had gone overseas on health-care missions, and there he was.

"His name is Morris Riker. In 2009, he made a trip to Africa to a little town called 'Durban' on the country's Indian Ocean coast."

"Once you had a name," I said, "I'm guessing you were able to trace his recent activities?"

"We were. Credit card receipts showed that he had been in the Kansas City area for several months, then suddenly, about the time we thought he went underground here, there were charges to a Super 8 motel in Goodland, Kansas."

Apparently, Mark Davenport had made

contact with Dr. Death.

"So where is he now?" Ox asked.

"He's back in Kansas City. A credit card charge just appeared at the Embassy Suites.

"Walt, this was your case. Do you and Ox want to bring him in?"

I had mixed feelings.

The man was a doctor, not a criminal.

He had done humanitarian work with the underprivileged in Africa, and, as far as I could see, his only crime was helping the terminally ill end their suffering.

But what could I say?

He had broken the law and if I didn't bring him in, somebody else would.

I figured it might as well be me. At least I could afford him the dignity that he deserved.

"Sure. We'll do it," I said.

On the way to the Embassy Suites, Ox said, "How do you want to handle this?"

"As delicately as possible. This guy isn't a scumbag."

"Shall we go for the old 'maintenance' ploy?"

"It's as good as any."

When we arrived at the hotel, we showed our badges at the front desk and got Riker's room number from the clerk.

We approached the door and knocked.

"Who is it?" came a voice from within.

"Maintenance!" Ox said. "We've had a report from the room below yours that there's a leak coming from your bathroom. We need to check it out."

"I'm terribly sorry," came the reply. "I can't come to the door right now. Maybe you could come back in a half hour."

"Can't do that," Ox said. "It's a pretty bad leak and it's ruining the apartment below."

"Well I'm afraid I can't let you in just now. It's terribly inconvenient."

Ox looked at me and I just shrugged my shoulders. I knew what he was going to do.

Ox took a deep breath and slammed his number twelve's into the door.

The jam splintered, the door flew open and what we saw was the last thing in the world that we expected to see.

Dr. Death was seated in an easy chair and a tube ran from the syringe in his arm to the Thanatron machine.

He was startled, but he didn't move.

When he saw that it was me, he smiled and said, "Good morning officer. Or should I call you Ray Braxton? You look a lot better than the last time we met."

225

"Dr. Riker! What are you doing?"

"I'm doing the same thing for myself that I've done for dozens of others. I am ending my pain and suffering and choosing to die with dignity."

"Pain and suffering? What are you talking about?" Ox asked.

"I'm dying, officer. In 2009, I contracted XDR tuberculosis when I was in Africa. Life expectancy is just two years and my time is about up."

He doubled over in a fit of coughing.

"I'm sorry to hear that," Ox said, "but we have orders to bring you in. You have broken the law."

"I wish you wouldn't do that. I only have a few weeks or maybe a month. I don't want to die in a cold jail cell or a prison hospital."

Ox started to protest but Riker interrupted.

"Mr. Braxton, or whatever your real name is, do you know why I didn't return that night to finish the job?"

"I've often wondered."

"I have looked into the eyes of a hundred dying patients and without fail, I could always see the longing for the peace that can only come from being released from this mortal shell.

"When I looked into your eyes that night, I

knew without a doubt that you were not ready to die."

I knew what he was talking about. I had seen that look in the eyes of the patients in the Kevorkian documentary. It was something that couldn't be mimicked.

"Look into my eyes, officer, and tell me what you see."

I looked and I saw his desperate cry for relief.

"Please," he pleaded. "If you would have been just thirty minutes later, it would have been done. Must I spend weeks in pain and agony for a mere thirty minutes?"

I looked at Ox and I know he could read my mind.

"It's your call, partner," he said.

"Dr. Riker, I know that you believe with all your heart that what you have been doing is right. I wish it were that easy for the rest of us.

"We're officers of the law and the law requires that justice be served, but justice can be served in many ways.

"Fate has dealt you a strange hand in that it has brought you to this moment where you will experience exactly what you have been giving others.

"If what you have been doing is righteous, then you will rest in the peace it brings. If not, you will know soon enough.

227

"Either way, I believe justice will be served."

"Thank you," he said. "That is all I ask."

"Then go in peace," I said.

We left the Embassy out the back entrance to avoid the desk clerk and drove several blocks away.

Ox parked and I took my pen and pressed it against the valve stem of the back tire.

As the air left the tire, I thought of the life leaving the body of Dr. Riker.

"Damn," I said to Ox. "Looks like we've got a flat tire. You'd better call it in."

Forty-five minutes later, the tire had been repaired and we were again standing at Dr. Riker's door.

We pushed it open and saw that the incredible saga of Dr. Death had come to an end.

The man that had called himself Thanatos had gone through the same portal as those who had sought him.

I wondered if he had found the peace that he so longed for.

I stared into his still face and saw that his lips were curled into a smile.

Maybe he had.

EPILOGUE

The capture of the two men that had tried to bring my law enforcement career to an end, along with our elderberry caper, focused new attention on the collusion between greedy corporate executives and corrupt public officials.

While our form of government is head and shoulders above any other, its success or failure is determined by the moral character of those elected to represent us.

When, out of greed and the lust for power, the public trust is violated, the very fabric of our society is put at risk.

Often, the battle against the rich and powerful seems futile and it is much easier to just look the other way, but sometimes the mighty are brought to their knees by the seemingly insignificant.

The classic illustration of that principle is H.G. Well's novel, *War Of The Worlds*.

The story is of a Martian invasion of the earth. Human weapons had proven useless against the powerful invaders and just when it appeared that all was lost, the Martians fell to microscopic bacteria to which humans were immune.

One can only hope that maybe something so

simple as an elderberry could be the catalyst that initiates the reform that will bring an end to the corruption and collusion that put our way of life at risk.

While the distinction between right and wrong is perfectly clear in some cases, it certainly isn't in others.

My encounter with Dr. Death is a case in point.

To some, he was an angel of mercy while to others his acts were those of a cold-blooded killer.

So many things in our lives beg for answers. Is it right or wrong? Is it good or evil? Is it true or false?

Euthanasia is just one of the conundrums of life.

Should we support gun control or every citizen's right to bear arms under the second amendment?

Should abortion be banned or should we support the right to choose?

What about gay marriage?

The thing that makes these choices so difficult is that there are men and women of goodwill who champion both sides.

A French author once wrote, "The only constant in life is change."

Less than a hundred years ago a black man couldn't drink from the same water fountain as a white man.

Today, we have a black president.

It's as certain as the sun coming up tomorrow, that public opinion on such issues will change.

Only history will decide if that change represents moral decay or moral enlightenment.

In the meantime, each of us has to make tough decisions in our daily lives.

Is it right or wrong for a man to take the life of another?

Every cop, every day, must make that decision when he buckles his gun belt around his waist.

The cop that pulls the trigger to save the life of a pregnant mother is a hero.

The cop that shoots a teenage boy whose cell phone was mistaken for a gun is a villain.

Same act, different circumstances.

I have taken a man's life in the performance of my duty, so I guess you could say that I have crossed that line.

The thing that allows me to sleep at night is Pastor Bob's words, "Circumstances alter cases."

I choose to believe, like Pastor Bob, that everything is not written in black and white, but in a thousand shades of gray.

Life would be easy if everything was absolute, but it's not.

Ox and I made the decision to walk away from Thanatos.

Was it the right thing to do?

Some would say not, but under that particular set of circumstances, I believed it was the right thing to do and I acted according to my heart.

Lady Justice is depicted wearing a blindfold and holding a balance scale.

Our lives are much like that of Lady Justice; we are blinded from knowing the absolute truth and yet, by the decisions we make every day, we try to maintain a balance between right and wrong.

When men of ill will make bad decisions and tip the scales of life in the direction of evil, someone has to step onto the side of good to bring the scales of life back into balance.

My name is Walter Williams and that's why I'm a cop!

LADY JUSTICE TAKES A. C.R.A.P.
City Retiree Action Patrol

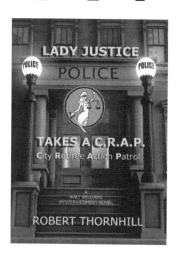

This is where it all began.

See how sixty-five year old Walt Williams became a cop and started the City Retiree Action Patrol.

Meet Maggie, Willie, Mary and the Professor, Walt's sidekicks in all of the Lady Justice novels.

Laugh out loud as Walt and his band of Senior Scrappers capture the Realtor Rapist and take down the Russian Mob.

http://booksbybob.com/lady-justice-takes-a-crap-3rd_383.html

LADY JUSTICE AND THE LOST TAPES

In *Lady Justice and the Lost Tapes*, Walt and his band of scrappy seniors continue their battle against the forces of evil.

When an entire Eastside Kansas City neighborhood is terrorized by the mob, Walt must go undercover to help solve the case.

Later, the amazing discovery of a previously unknown recording session by a deceased rock 'n' roll idol stuns the music industry.

http://booksbybob.com/lady-justice-and-the-lost-tapes_307.html

LADY JUSTICE GETS LEI'D

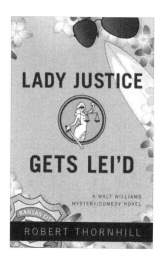

In *Lady Justice Gets Lei'd*, Walt and Maggie plan a romantic honeymoon on the beautiful Hawaiian islands, but ancient artifacts discovered in a cave in a dormant volcano and a surprising revelation about Maggie's past, lead our lovers into the hands of Hawaiian zealots.

http://booksbybob.com/lady-justice-gets-leid_309.html

LADY JUSTICE
AND THE AVENGING ANGELS

Lady Justice has unwittingly entered a religious war. Who better to fight for her than Walt Williams?

The Avenging Angels believe it's their job to rain fire and brimstone on Kansas City, their Sodom and Gomorrah.

In this compelling addition to the Lady Justice series, Robert Thornhill brings back all the characters readers have come to love for more hilarity and higher stakes.

You'll laugh, and you'll be on the edge of your seat until the big finish.

Don't miss *Lady Justice and the Avenging Angels*!

http://booksbybob.com/lady-justice-and-the-avenging-angels_336.html

LADY JUSTICE AND THE STING

BEST NEW MYSTERY NOVEL ---WINTER 2012

National Association of Book Entrepreneurs

In *Lady Justice and the Sting*, a holistic physician is murdered and Walt becomes entangled in the high-powered world of pharmaceutical giants and corrupt politicians.

Maggie, Ox Willie, Mary and all your favorite characters are back to help Walt bring the criminals to justice in the most unorthodox ways.

A dead-serious mystery with hilarious twists!

http://booksbybob.com/lady-justice-and-the-sting_348.html

LADY JUSTICE AND DR. DEATH

BEST NEW MYSTERY NOVEL --- FALL 2011

National Association of Book Entrepreneurs

In *Lady Justice and Dr. Death*, a series of terminally ill patients are found dead under circumstances that point to a new Dr. Death practicing euthanasia in the Kansas City area.

Walt and his entourage of scrappy seniors are dragged into the 'right-to-die-with-dignity' controversy.

The mystery provides a light-hearted look at this explosive topic and death in general.

You may see end-of-life issues in a whole new light after reading *Lady Justice and Dr. Death*!

http://booksbybob.com/lady-justice-and-dr-death_351.html

238

LADY JUSTICE AND THE VIGILANTE

BEST NEW MYSTERY NOVEL – SUMMER 2012

National Association of Book Entrepreneurs

A vigilante is stalking the streets of Kansas City administering his own brand of justice when the justice system fails.

Criminals are being executed right under the noses of the police department.

A new recruit to the City Retiree Action Patrol steps up to help Walt and Ox bring an end to his reign of terror.

But not everyone wants the vigilante stopped. His bold reprisals against the criminal element have inspired the average citizen to take up arms and defend themselves.

As the body count mounts, public opinion is split.

Is it justice or is it murder?

A moral dilemma that will leave you laughing and weeping!

http://booksbybob.com/lady-justice-and-the-vigilante_362.html

239

LADY JUSTICE AND THE WATCHERS

Suzanne Collins wrote *The Hunger Games*, Aldous Huxley wrote *Brave New World* and George Orwell wrote *1984*.

All three novels were about dystopian societies of the future.

In *Lady Justice and the Watchers*, Walt sees the world we live in today through the eyes of a group who call themselves 'The Watchers'.

Oscar Levant said that there's a fine line between genius and insanity.

After reading *Lady Justice and the Watchers*, you may realize as Walt did that there's also a fine line separating the life of freedom that we enjoy today and the totalitarian society envisioned in these classic novels.

Quietly and without fanfare, powerful interests have instituted policies that have eroded our privacy, health and individual freedoms.

Is the dystopian society still a thing of the distant future or is it with us now disguised as a wolf in sheep's clothing?

http://booksbybob.com/lady-justice-and-the-watchers_365.html

LADY JUSTICE AND THE CANDIDATE

BEST NEW MYSTERY NOVEL – FALL 2012

National Association of Book Entrepreneurs

Will American politics always be dominated by the two major political parties or are voters longing for an Independent candidate to challenge the establishment?

Everyone thought that the slate of candidates for the presidential election had been set until Benjamin Franklin Foster came on the scene capturing the hearts of American voters with his message of change and reform.

Powerful interests intent on preserving the status quo with their bought-and-paid-for politicians were determined to take Ben Foster out of the race.

The Secret Service comes up with a quirky plan to protect the Candidate and strike a blow for Lady Justice.

Join Walt on the campaign trail for an adventure full of surprises, mystery, intrigue and laughs!

http://booksbybob.com/lady-justice-and-the-candidate_367.html

LADY JUSTICE AND THE BOOK CLUB MURDERS

Best New Mystery Novel – Spring 2013

Members of the Midtown Book Club are found murdered.

It is just the beginning of a series of deaths that lead Walt and Ox into the twisted world of a serial killer.

In the late 1960's, the Zodiac Killer claimed to have killed 37 people and was never caught --- the perfect crime.

Oscar Roach, dreamed of being the next serial killer to commit the perfect crime.

He left a calling card with each of his victims --- a mystery novel, resting in their blood-soaked hands.

The media dubbed him 'The Librarian'.

Walt and the Kansas City Police are baffled by the cunning of this vicious killer and fear that he has indeed committed the perfect crime.

Or did he?

Walt and his wacky senior cohorts prove, once again, that life goes on in spite of the carnage around them.

The perfect blend of murder, mayhem and merriment.

http://booksbybob.com/lady-justice-and-the-book-club-murders_370.html

LADY JUSTICE AND THE
CRUISE SHIP MURDERS

Ox and Judy are off to Alaska on a honeymoon cruise and invite Walt and Maggie to tag along.

Their peaceful plans are soon shipwrecked by the murder of two fellow passengers.

The murders appear to be linked to a century-old legend involving a cache of gold stolen from a prospector and buried by two thieves.

Their seven-day cruise is spent hunting for the gold and eluding the modern day thieves intent on possessing it at any cost.

Another nail-biting mystery that will have you on the edge of your seat one minute and laughing out loud the next.

http://booksbybob.com/lady-justice-and-the-cruise-ship-murders_373.html

243

LADY JUSTICE
AND THE
CLASS REUNION

For most people, a 50th class reunion is a time to party and renew old acquaintances, but Walt Williams isn't an ordinary guy --- he's a cop, and trouble seems to follow him everywhere he goes.

The Mexican drug cartel is recruiting young Latino girls as drug mules and the Kansas City Police have hit a brick wall until Walt is given a lead by an old classmate.

Even then, it takes three unlikely heroes from the Whispering Hills Retirement Village to help Walt and Ox end the cartel's reign of terror.

Join Walt in a class reunion filled with mystery, intrigue, jealousy and a belly-full of laughs!
http://booksbybob.com/lady-justice-and-the-class-reunion_387.html

LADY JUSTICE AND THE ASSASSIN

Two radical groups have joined together for a common purpose --- to kill the President of the United States, and they're looking for the perfect person to do the job.

Not a cold-blooded killer or a vicious assassin, but a model citizen, far removed from the watchful eyes of Homeland Security.

When the president comes to Kansas City, the unlikely trio of Walt, Willie and Louie the Lip find themselves knee-deep in the planned assassination.

Join our heroes for another suspenseful mystery and lots of laughs!

http://booksbybob.com/lady-justice-and-the-assassin_395.html

WOLVES IN SHEEP'S CLOTHING

In August of 2011, I completed the fifth novel in the *Lady Justice* mystery/comedy series, *Lady Justice And The Sting*.

As I always do, I sent copies of the completed manuscript to several friends and acquaintances for their feedback and comments before sending the manuscript to the publisher.

Since the plot involved a holistic physician, I sent a copy to Dr. Edward Pearson in Florida.

Dr. Pearson loved the premise of the book and the style of writing, particularly as it related to alternative healthcare, natural products and Walt's transformation into a healthier lifestyle.

246

In subsequent conversations, Dr. Pearson shared that he had been looking for a book that he could share with his patients, colleagues and peers that would spread his message in a format that would capture their imagination and their hearts.

The Sting was very close to what he had been looking for and he made the suggestion that maybe we could work together to produce just the right book.

As I reflected on this idea, I realized that Walt's skirmishes with pharmaceutical companies, corrupt politicians, doctors, nurses, hospitals, bodily afflictions and a healthier lifestyle were not confined to just *The Sting*, but were scattered throughout all six of the *Lady Justice* mystery/comedy novels.

Using *The Sting* as the basis of the new book, I went through the manuscripts of the other five *Lady Justice* novels and pulled out chapters and vignettes that fleshed out the story of Walt's medical adventures.

Thus, *Wolves In Sheep's Clothing* was born.

Dr. Pearson is currently using *Wolves* in conjunction with his New Medicine Foundation to help spread the word about healthcare alternatives.

New Medicine Foundation
Dr. Edward W. Pearson, MD, ABIHM
http://newmedicinefoundation.com

RAINBOW ROAD
CHAPTER BOOKS FOR CHILDREN
AGES 5 – 10

Super Secrets of Rainbow Road

Super Powers of Rainbow Road

Hawaiian Rainbows

Patriotic Rainbows

Sports Heroes of Rainbow Road

Ghosts and Goblins of Rainbow Road

Christmas Crooks of Rainbow Road

For more information,
Go to http://BooksByBob.com

ABOUT THE AUTHOR

Award-winning author, Robert Thornhill, began writing at the age of sixty-six, and in four short years has penned thirteen novels in the Lady Justice mystery/comedy series, the seven volume Rainbow Road series of chapter books for children, a cookbook and a mini-autobiography.

The fifth, sixth, seventh, ninth and tenth novels in his Lady Justice series, *Lady Justice and the Sting, Lady Justice and Dr. Death, Lady Justice and the Vigilante, Lady Justice and the Candidate* and *Lady Justice and the Book Club Murders* won the Pinnacle Achievement Award from the National Association of Book Entrepreneurs as the best mystery novels in 2011, 2012 and 2013.

Robert holds a master's degree in psychology, but his wit and insight come from his varied occupations including thirty years as a real estate broker.

He lives with his wife, Peg, in Independence, Mo.

5220368R00135

Made in the USA
San Bernardino, CA
30 October 2013